THOSE PESKY GOBLINZ

A Game About Deep, Dark, and Dismal Creatures
By Justin LaNasa

1st Edition
Role-Playing Game

Cover Art Qwerty / Coloring by Mick McArt
Interior Art by Qwerty, Jesse Hansen, Chris Lesley, Josh Pinero, Kylie Jones, Dean Spencer, William McAusland, Joe Ernst, & Jim Holloway
Design & Layout by Mick McArt

Dedication by Ernest G. Gygax Jr.

THOSE PESKY GOBLINZ
by Justin LaNasa
Copyright 2021 by TSR LLC. All rights reserved.

This book may not be reproduced or transmitted in any form or by any means, electronic or mechanical. Including photocopying recordings or any other information storage and retrieval system without the written permission of the author.

ISBN 978-1-7341961-4-6

Published by Mick Art Productions, LLC.

Special thanks to the Troll Godfather

DEDICATION

In humble honor and respect to the teachings of the highest-level Game Master of the 20th Century. My father, E. Gary Gygax.

First, by example, playing Avalon Hill Games and leaving them where an infant could use his walker and thereby reach up to cut his first tooth on a SS Panzer Division (Stalingrad game). Then further by example, he wrote rules variants and what-ifs for assorted newsletters, even doing self-published sheets, using Fireman's Fund Insurance tools from his employment, to spread gaming to areas outside Chicago and the Lake Geneva area. Later by simple game instruction, layer by layer, adding difficulty and longevity to the equation. First Tic Tac Toe, then Checkers, Chinese Checkers, Stratego, Chess, Feudal, Battle of the Bulge (AH), Ancients Rome versus Carthage, Fort Sahara, Tractics WWII (Airx miniatures). Then Napoleonics, English Civil War, American Civil War (25mm lead armies). Then Chainmail using 40mm Elastolin's on our sand table.

He took me to Chicago to meet his International Federation of Wargamers associates and then invited the same to our home. The gathering was a complete success to the dozen attendees but almost cost Gary his happy home. So next year, he organized through the IFW the first Geneva Convention (Gen Con 1968). Gary always welcomed individual gamers to our home with no more knowledge of each except that they were fellow game players seeking others of similar ilk. Mike Webster brought his car, drum set, Ruffles potato chips, and Pepsi Cola to our home. He lived on our screen porch for summer.

With his childhood pal Don Kaye, Gary built a six by 10 ft Sand table in our basement. Then they founded the Castle & Crusades Society, a gaming community meeting at least weekly at our house to play miniature games on the Sand table. The sand table later had to move to Don's garage after Dad lost his Insurance Underwriting position, and after many humble but difficult tries, he settled on Shoe Cobbling at home. Due to a loan from his mother for the equipment. Almina (grandmother) was my father's lifeline when things became difficult. While this trade barely kept the family afloat, often generating less than $100 a week. He found time to share his newfound profession with my brother Luke and me. I even learned cobbling skills to create "Ho Chi Min" +sandals for the local Monastery from leather and Goodyear tire material.

Then and only after writing or assisting in the creation of miniatures rules for Conanomacy, Indianomacy (Diplomacy variants), Napoleonics (Tricolor), Napoleonic Naval action (DGUTS), English Civil War (C&R), Civil War Naval (Ironclad), World War II man to man (Tractics), Medieval with the Fantasy supplement (Chainmail). He created the board games Dunkirk, Alexander, and the Battle of Little Bighorn. Then after years of correspondence and gaming conventions working from the 20-odd pages of notes from Dave Arneson, Gary wrote, formed a partnership, and published the boxed original Dungeons & Dragons game through Tactical Studies Rules (TSR). He involved me in every step of these various works, often to little immediate reward due to my youth. Yet he never wavered to me or anyone who wished to come together to play a game.

He led me to Robert E. Howard at the age of 10. Thereby taking me from one who faked book reports and transforming me into an avid devourer of action, be it war, fantasy, or science. Ernest Gary Gygax did not follow the path most traveled; he was a rebel believing that imagination is far more rewarding than perspiration. Yet when it came down to sharing and putting that imagination into a shared venue, he never stinted on the efforts, often falling asleep at his typewriter. At the same time, his lovely young wife slept in the marital bed alone for far too many nights. Every time we play either a role-playing game or a computer game with a leveling/reward system, air units have a part in board games…. I and all of us owe to the efforts and groundbreaking activities that we all take for granted. We all owe this debt to the Father of Gaming and Role-Playing E. Gary Gygax 1938-2008.

Ernest Gary Gygax, Jr.

THE ISLAND OF THE FAY
BY EDGAR ALLAN POE

The Island of the Fay.

SCIENCE, true daughter of old Time thou art,

Who alterest all things with thy peering eyes!

Why prey'st thou thus upon the poet's heart,

Vulture, whose wings are dull realities?

How should he love thee, or how deem thee wise,

Who wouldst not leave him, in his wandering,

To seek for treasure in the jewelled skies,

Albeit be soared with an undaunted wing?

Hast thou not dragged Diana from her car?

And driven the Hamadryad from the wood?

Hast thou not spoilt a story in each star?

Hast thou not torn the Naiad from her flood?

The elfin from the grass? — the dainty fay,

The witch, the sprite, the goblin — where are they? Anon.

FOREWORD

My name is Justin LaNasa I have been playing role-playing games since 1980. I started playing at our local library every Saturday morning and at our local game store. The Order Line in York, Pennsylvania. We played all kinds of role-playing games, board games, and miniature battles, and yes, I learned how to paint miniatures on a large and small scale; those were the days of High Imagination. And yes, I went through the so-called days of Satanic Panic. Yes, I had many copies of my Dungeons & Dragons Books Burnt. I even remember being banned from the Order Line by my parents and having to sit on their back-porch gaming through the screen door that was acceptable by the store owners, Mr. Potter & Mr. Strickler.

Hopefully, no one will ever consider this game or any other role-playing game a tool of Evil or Satanic. I can credit Dungeons & Dragons and the multitude of games we played for helping me read and expand my creativity, tactics, teamwork, and problem-solving skills. It also kept me off the streets and out of trouble as a teenager.

Hopefully, you and your family can benefit from this form of role-playing. Bringing your family closer and forming the bond as it did with us. I 'am still good friends with most of the original gamers we gamed with and have made new lifelong friends through gaming. I also encourage you to try other role-playing games as your family grows in experience with Goblinz.

Thank you all

Justin LaNasa

INTRODUCTION

Goblins are a tribal society. They often dwell in deep, dark, dismal, underground places, like dungeons. They hate daylight and attack at a -1 to hit while in sunlight. Goblins have an infravision of 60' range. They have a racial hatred for gnomes and dwarves and will attack them at any opportunity. Some goblins may also be found in deep dark forests, jungles, and forgotten ruins. Goblins have been used as servants or minions by hobgoblins, orcs, gnolls, ogres, and trolls for as long as memories exist.

For this game, you are playing the anomaly of your goblin kind. You are bigger, stronger, and able to gain levels and abilities unlike other average goblins.

Goblins, while evil, still have an orderly or honorable sense of being, but only to other goblins. These creatures will steal, cheat, or lie to any other non-goblinoids. Goblins love silver and gold and any type of jewels.

They love to eat raw food found underground or in forests. Insects and grubs are their favorite natural delicacies. They love raiding villages at night to steal whatever supplies they can get their hands on. Goblins would even eat members of other races, including goblinoids like kobolds, orcs, ogres, and trolls. Trolls are a treat to have in the icebox. They keep regenerating to produce more food but need to be kept a close eye on not to allow Mr. Troll to regenerate fully and make a meal of you. Goblins will only eat other goblins as a last resort.

What goblins fear the most is horse blood; dogs are also disliked. The goblins seem to get along well with Wolves & Worgs, though. Goblins reach adulthood by age eight and can live to approximately 50 years if lucky. Female goblins are known as Goblettes. Goblins are known to ride anything they can get their hands on or train; giant spiders, giant toads, giant rats, boars, worgs, and carrion crawlers are a few.

It is well known that the Goblin King is of a particular breed, much like your breed. All goblins can speak Goblin, Evil, Kobold, Orcish, and Hobgoblin, and some have mastered other languages such as common, dwarven, and gnomish. Goblins consider kobolds a lesser servant-type race and tend to treat kobolds as pets rather than slaves.

The blood that runs through your goblin veins is unique. You always knew you weren't like the rest of your pack. You may choose the path of a warrior, wizard, shaman, or rogue.

CHARACTER CREATION

Start by rolling on the Trait Chart below, then on the Background Chart on page 9. Once you have determined your goblin's traits and background, you now roll 2D6 for each attribute on page 14. Arrange the numbers how you would like on your character sheet.

The breed is goblin unless you role something special on the traits chart. Buy extra equipment on page 15, and then pick your spells if you were lucky enough to get them. Write down your saving throws & roll hit points. Write down your ability modifiers. Create a name. Pick a Deity if a Shaman or a religious goblin you may be. Alignment as an average Goblin, most are Lawful Evil, only being Lawful to other goblinoids races like orcs, kobolds, hobgoblins, gnolls & ogres. You may be any combination of Lawful, Chaotic, Natural, or Evil, but your goblin may not be any form of good at the start.

TRAITZ

d20	Type	Description
1	Roll Twice	Roll twice on this chart. Keep both rolls as traits. If another one is rolled, add another trait roll. Stack if continued.
2	Pure White Goblin	A natural wizard. Can be dual class or gains double experience as a wizard. +1 INT. -20% to Hide. These goblins taste good so most other beings want to eat or attack them.
3	Carapace	A thick shell on your torso. Skin is thicker as well. Natural AC of splint mail. Movement is reduced by half.
4	Aquatic Goblin	Goblin has gills and semi-webbed feet and hands. You can breath water and move freely as you do on land. Diet is mainly fish or other aquatic creatures.
5	Claws	Goblin has claws that do 1D6 damage each. Goblin may climb walls and surfaces as the same level rogue.
6	Shorter	Half the height of a normal goblin, thus harder to hit. Attackers get -2 to all to hit rolls. Due to shorter legs, the goblins movement is reduced to 3/4 of a normal goblin.
7	Regeneration	A troll must have been in the family tree. Regenerate 1HP every 3 rounds. Goblin will regenerate back to life, but not if killed by fire.
8	Monster Appetite	Goblin has an insatiable appetite. Can and will eat everything looking tasty. +1 CON. Goblin is also immune to disease and poison. Movement is reduced to 1/2 due to obesity.
9	Bounce	Goblins skin and body is extremely rubbery. Goblin can fall from any distance with no damage. Goblin then bounces 1D10 feet after impact. Impossible to bind with bonds or keep in a cell.
10	Unnaturally Strong	Unnaturally strong with good stamina. During character creation, roll 3D6 for STR and CON. Goblin has aggressive bullyish behavior that others disdain.
11	Unnaturally Smarter	Unnatural intelligence and wisdom. During character creation, roll 3D6 for INT and WIS. Goblin has a know-it-all personality trait and will fight to the death to prove they are right, even if they are wrong.
12	Taller	Exceptionally tall for a goblin. 4ft + 1D4 feet in height. Uses a D8 for HD and moves 1/4 faster than normal goblins.
13	Pure Black Goblin	Even this goblins blood is black. Hide +20%. Shunned by most other goblins, they are favored by orcs and ogres who use them for personal guards and assassins. X2 exp. if a rogue and start with +2GP. Monsters hate taste of these goblins flesh. If swallowed whole there is a 50% chance they will be spit out unharmed).
14	Horned Goblin	1D2 horns on their skull that can do 1D6 damage. Helmets cost X2 due to having to be customized.
15	Bump of Direction	Goblin's ability to sense true north is 95% accurate. A natural caver and cartographer who never gets lost. Can detect shifting walls or secret doors with elf-like ability.
16	Spined Goblin	Possesses 6 spines growing down their back. When frightened the goblin can launch any number of these up to 20 feet. Each spine does 1d3 damage upon successful hit. Regrows 1 spine every 12 hours.
17	Unnaturally Weak	Goblin is super weak when creating character. Roll only a 1D6 for STR and CON. On the plus side, other goblins pity them, have low expectations, and keep them out of their drama, which usually means they tend to live longer.
18	Unnaturally Fast	Goblin is super fast. Movement speed x2, 2 attacks per round. High metabolism requires goblin to eat large amounts of meat/flesh.
19	Winged Goblin	Partial wings allow this goblin to glide (at normal movement), and have normal flight (at 1/4 normal movement). Armor costs are double due to customization.
20	Sired by Ogre	Sired by an ogre this special goblin is now a Hobgoblin. All scores are rolled using 3D6. Max class levels are 13. HD is 1D8+1. Born leader of goblins and always chosen as such. Starting money is gold, not copper.

BACKGROUNDZ

d20	Goblin Type	Abilities	Equipment & Heirlooms	Copper Pieces
1	Alchemist	Beginner's Alchemy (make a Healing Potion in 1 week for 100cp)	1 Healing potion, mortar and pestle	2D6
2	Noble	+1 hit/dam. Short sword. Trust: 1D6gp per week. Goblin Etiquette.	Signet ring, chain mail, long sword, and horse	2D6 GP
3	Worg Trainer	Animal Handling (+4 Reaction Roll for Worgs and other animals)	Chicken, baby worg (1HD, AC7, 1D6 bite)	2D6
4	Archer	Rapid Fire (fires arrows twice per round if not moving or in melee)	Long bow, quiver, 15 arrows, 5 silver arrows	2D6
5	Bandit	Evasion (flee combat without being hit, but only if wearing leather armor)	Hooded cloak, leather armor, shield, short bow, quiver, 20 arrows, treasure map (ruin)	2D6
6	Barkeep	Ear for Listening (knows 2D6 local rumors)	Flask of fine spirits (50cp value, +2 Reaction Roll if a shot is offered, 10 shots total	2D6
7	Berserker	Rage (+2 to attack rolls & AC7 if no armor, will not flee or surrender), +1HP per level	Bearskin cloak, tooth-bitten shield	1D6
8	Buccaneer	Swimming (-20% chance of drowning), ship-craft, rope use	Cutlass, spyglass, treasure map (island), pet monkey (1HP), 50' rope with grappling hook	3D6
9	Cave	Tough (+1HD at 1st level, but will not wear any armor), hunting, illiterate	Furs, club or stone axe and spear, hide sack with meat and fruit	---
10	Engineer	Eye for Construction (detect dungeon traps as a dwarf and secret doors as an elf)	Lantern, steel mirror, chalk stick, level, measuring stick (6', ruled)	3D6
11	Slaver	Command ability on all kobolds while holding whip. Save to resist	Whip, shackles, leather armor, 1D4 kobold slaves	3D6
12	Gemcutter	Appraise (gems and jewelry), cut gems (4 in 6 chance of increasing value of a gem by 10%)	Magnifying lens, diamond dust (50cp value, use 10cp per attempt to cut gem)	2D6
13	Sentry	Years of Guard Duty (surprised only on 1 in 6)	Chain mail, shield, sword, dagger, light crossbow, 30 quarrels in case	2D6
14	Chef	The ability to turn most anything into a tasty meal. +1 Hit/Damage with knives and daggers	Leather apron AC8, butcher knife, cooking pot, 1D6 spices	1D6
15	Nomad	Surprise Outdoors (1-4 in 6, if wearing only leather armor), Archery while Riding	Light horse, lance, horse bow, leather armor	1D6
16	Merchant	Trader bartering abilities(May buy items at 1/2 normal prices) +1 to CHA	Leather armor, shield, hand axe	3D6
17	Gypsy	Traveling (add 1 hex to daily movement)	Sturdy staff, holy relic (turns undead as 3rd level cleric 2D6 times before disintegrating)	2D6
18	Sage	Identify Magic Item (takes 1 week and uses 100cp of material components)	Reference books, blank vellum book, ink and quill	2D6
19	Smith	Fire-touch (-1 point per dice fire damage), Forging (make weapons /armor at 1/2 cost)	Chain mail, shield, hammer, tongs, 12 iron spikes, crowbar	2D6
20	Spy	Double Talk (+2 on Reaction Rolls), Disguise, Language (double normal number)	2 daggers (1 hidden in book)	2D6

Each background also gets a +2 Reaction Roll when encountering other of the same background.

ABBREVIATION KEY

Throughout this book you will see lot's of abbreviations. We are listing them here for your reference.

GM - Goblin Master	STR - Strength	- LG - Lawful Good	GP - Gold Pieces
PC - Player Character	INT - Intelligence	- NG - Neutral Good	PP - Platinum Pieces
NPC- Non-Player Character	WIS - Wisdom	- CG Chaotic Good	EP - Electrum Pieces
AC - Armor Class	DEX - Dexterity	- N - Neutral	SP - Silver Pieces
HP - Hit Points	CON - Constitution	- LE - Lawful Evil	CP - Copper Pieces
HD - Hit Dice	CHA - Charisma	- NE - Neutral Evil	ATR - Attributes
	AL - Alignment	- CE - Chaotic Evil	

DIE ROLL TO SCORE A HIT (USE 1D20)

Level			THAC10	9	8	7	6	5	4	3	2	1	0	Opponent HD
Warrior	Shaman/ Rogue	Wizard		None	Leather			Chain		Plate				
		Normal Goblin	12	11	12	13	14	15	16	17	18	19	20	
1-3	1-4	1-5	11	10	11	12	13	14	15	16	17	18	19	up to 1
			10	9	10	11	12	13	14	15	16	17	18	1+ to 2
4-6	5-8	6-10	9	8	9	10	11	12	13	14	15	16	17	2+ to 3
	9-10		7	6	7	8	9	10	11	12	13	14	15	3+ to 4
7-8			6	5	6	7	8	9	10	11	12	13	14	4+ to 6+
9-10			5	4	5	6	7	8	9	10	11	12	13	7 (9HD+4 11HD+6)

INITIATIVE

To determine who gets first attack in combat, initiative must be rolled. Roll 1D6, then add your goblin's reaction adjustment from dexterity.

PIVOT POINTS (Gygaxian Game Play Lore)

These points are earned and given by the GM by doing fantastic or incredibly heroic feats that may have no more than the character's level. If used before the die roll, it can change the outcome drastically by just saying I'm using a pivot point to keep the Knight from slicing me with his flaming sword. But if used after the die rolls, it will give a +4 modifier in favor of the user. You may use Pivot Points for other characters if within sight. Characters start with 1 Pivot Point.

THAC10

To determine a hit use the **To Hit Armor Class 10** system. To hit refer to the **Die Roll To Score A Hit** chart above. Example A: 1 HD opponent to hit ac 10 need a 11 or greater on a 20 side die.

BLIND FIGHTING

Characters fight with a -4 to hit if totally blind, or a -2 if partially blind.

GOBLIN ARMOR

Type	AC Rating
Prone	10
None	9
Turtle Shell Shield / Animal Hide	8
Animal Hide or Leather + shield/Alligator Skin	7
Alligator Skin +Shield / Piece Meal Armor	6
Piece Meal Armor + Shield / Rickety Splint Mail or Chain Mail	5
Rickety Splint or Chain Mail + Shield / Iron Wood Piece Mail	4
Iron Wood Piece Mail + Shield / Iron Wood Plate Mail	3
Dragon Scale Piece Mail / Iron Wood Plate Mail	2

OPPONENT HIT DICE

Under 1	Peasants, Villagers
1-3+	Veterans, Conjurers, Adepts, Robbers
4-6+	Heros, Magician, Bishops, Sharper
7-9+	Champions, Warlocks
10-12+	Super Heroes, Necromancers
13-15+	Lords, Patriarchs, Master Thieves

Warrior

"Killing small group of humans was easy," Boleg the Circler bragged to his team, wiping off his blade. "Me just glad they wuz' asleep, or the battle would have been much harder!"

As a Warrior, your prime attribute is strength, so the higher, the better. As a warrior, you may wear any armor if it fits your 4ft height and stature.

L	Title	Exp	+Hit/Dm	HD
0	Normal Goblin	0		1D7
1	Enlisted Goblin	0		1D8+1
2	Fighter Goblin	1500	+1	2D8
3	Backer Goblin	3000		3D8
4	Guardian Goblin	6000	+2	4D8
5	Protector Goblin	12000		5D8
6	Vanquisher Goblin	24000	+3	6D8
7	Conqueror Goblin	48000		7D8
8	Subduer Goblin	96000	+4	8D8
9	Incarcerator Goblin	192000		9D8+2
10	Overlord Goblin	292000	+5	9D8+4

SAVING THROWS (1d20)					
LV	Poison	Wand	Stone	Breath	Spell
1	13	14	15	16	17
2	12	13	14	15	16
3	12	13	14	15	16
4	12	13	14	15	16
5	10	11	12	13	14
6	10	11	12	13	14
7	10	11	12	13	14
8	8	9	10	10	12
9	6	7	8	8	10
10	4	5	5	5	8

Wizard

Flames shot from the goblin's magically glowing hands, engulfing the flesh before him! "Feel the might of Mungbar!" the goblin wizard shouted.

"You burnt food again," another goblin complained, throwing down his plate by the campfire.

"Sorry," Mungbar shrugged. "Me get carried away."

As a Wizard, your prime attribute is intelligence. To be a wizard, you must have a minimum INT of 9. As a wizard, you are limited to no armor (beware).

L	Title	Exp	HD	Spells
1	Augur Goblin	0	1D4	1
2	Soothsayer Goblin	2000	2D4	2
3	Mystic Goblin	4000	3D4	2-1
4	Foreteller Goblin	8000	4D4	4-2
5	Diviner Goblin	16000	5D4	4-2-1
6	Charmer Goblin	32000	6D4	4-2-2
7	Occultist Goblin	64000	7D4	4-3-2-1
8	Hypnotist Goblin	128000	8D4	4-3-2-2
9	Magnus Goblin	200000	9D4	4-3-3-2-1
10	Magi Goblin	300000	10D4	4-3-3-2-2

SAVING THROWS (1d20)					
Level	Poison	Wand	Stone	Breath	Spell
1	13	14	13	16	15
2	13	14	13	16	15
3	13	14	13	16	15
4	13	14	13	16	15
5	13	14	13	16	15
6	11	12	11	14	12
7	11	12	11	14	12
8	11	12	11	14	12
9	11	12	11	14	12
10	9	10	10	12	9

Shaman

Kwak the Shaman loved befriending the undead. Not only did they fight beside him when raiding ugly humans, but they were lousy at cards! Well, except for the vampires, who you know to let win. You may get rich, but chances are you'll stumble away feeling compeletely drained.

Level	Title	Exp	HD	Spells
1	Aid Goblin	0	1D8	1
2	Helper Goblin	1000	2D8	1
3	Padre Goblin	2000	3D8	2
4	Pastor Goblin	4000	4D8	2-1
5	Minister Goblin	8000	5D8	2-2
6	Healer Goblin	16000	6D8	2-2-1-1
7	Voodoo Goblin	32000	7D8	2-2-2-1-1
8	Shaman Goblin	64000	8D8	2-2-2-2-2

SHAMAN SAVING THROWS

Level	Poison	Wand	Stone	Breath	Spell
1	11	12	14	16	15
2	11	12	14	16	15
3	11	12	14	16	15
4	11	12	14	16	15
5	9	10	12	14	12
6	9	10	12	14	12
7	9	10	12	14	12
8	9	10	12	14	12

Professor Gobby says:
As a Shaman, your prime attribute is wisdom. To be a shaman, you must have a minimum WIS of 9. As a Shaman, you may wear armor attuned to the god you worship.

BEFRIEND UNDEAD (use 2D6)

Level	SK	ZO	GH	WI	WR	MU	VA	SP
1	7	9	11					
2	B	7	9	11				
3	B	B	7	9	11			
4	C	B	B	7	9	11		
5	C	C	B	B	7	9	11	
6	C	C	C	B	B	7	9	11
7	C	C	C	C	B	B	7	9
8	C	C	C	C	C	B	B	7

Befriend=2D8 Undead   Control=1D8+1 Undead

Befriend: undead creature is your friend but you will have to interact with the creature to have it do things for you. It may protect you from enemies but may retreat if it feels it might die or become overpowered.
Control: means total control of actions of the undead.

Rogue

Sneaking up on the cloaked creature wasn't easy, but Glopsup did it like a mouse swiping cheese from a trap. The backstab went well, as the creature before him dropped the sack of gold and fell silent. "Look everyone," he proclaimed. "Me killed their leader!"

"That was our leader, you dolt!" one of the goblins declared, before pausing and looking around. "Let's split the loot!"

L	Title	Exp	HD	Backstab +4 to hit
1	Lowlife Goblin	0	1D6	X2
2	Hooligan Goblin	800	2D6	X2
3	Mischief Goblin	1600	3D6	X2
4	Trickster Goblin	3200	4D6	X2
5	Scalawag Goblin	6400	5D6	X3
6	Scoundrel Goblin	12800	6D6	X3
7	Plunderer Goblin	25600	7D6	X3
8	Bandit Goblin	51200	8D6	X3
9	Hijacker Goblin	102400	9D6	X4
10	Marauder Goblin	204800	10D6	X4

As a Rogue, your prime attribute is dexterity. Rogues may only wear light armor.

Other than thieving skills, you are a master at disguise and poisons.

Professor Gobby says: A failed Make Poison attempt (if you have the proper components) will result in a DEX check on a D20 under your DEX. If failed save vs. the poison per effects of poison you were trying to make, then the batch is ruined.

ROGUE SAVING THROWS					
LV	Poison	Wand	Stone	Breath	Spell
1	12	13	14	15	16
2	12	13	14	15	16
3	12	13	14	15	16
4	10	11	12	13	14
5	10	11	12	13	14
6	10	11	12	13	14
7	8	9	10	10	12
8	8	9	10	10	12
9	8	9	10	10	12
10	6	7	8	8	10

Level	Disguise	Identify Poison	Make Poison
1	50%	20%	30%
2	55%	25%	30%
3	60%	30%	35%
4	65%	35%	40%
5	70%	40%	45%
6	75%	45%	50%
7	80%	50%	55%
8	85%	55%	60%
9	90%	60%	65%
10	95%	65%	70%

ROGUE ABILITIES (use percentage dice)							
Level	Open Locks	Find/Remove Traps	Pick Pocket	Move Silent	Hide in Shadows	Climb Walls	Hear Noise	Read Languages
1	15	10	20	20	10	87	1-2	
2	20	15	25	25	15	88	1-2	
3	25	20	30	30	20	89	1-3	
4	35	30	35	35	25	90	1-3	80
5	40	35	45	45	35	91	1-3	80
6	45	40	55	55	45	92	1-3	80
7	55	50	60	60	50	93	1-4	80
8	65	60	65	65	55	94	1-4	80
9	75	70	75	75	65	95	1-4	80
10	85	80	85	85	75	96	1-4	80

ATTRIBUTES

STRENGTH

Ability Score	Hit Probability	Damage Adjustment	Weight Allowance	Open Doors On A	Bend Bars/Lift Gates
2-3	-3	-1	-350	1	0%
4-5	-2	-1	-250	1	0%
6-7	-1	None	-150	1	0%
8-9	Normal	None	Normal	1-2	1%
10-11	Normal	None	Normal	1-2	2%
12-13	Normal	None	+100	1-2	4%
14-15	Normal	None	+200	1-2	7%
16	Normal	+1	+350	1-3	10%
17	+1	+1	+500	1-3	13%
18	+1	+2	+750	1-3	16%

INTELLIGENCE

Ability Score	Know Spell %	Min # of Spells/Level	Max # of Spells/Level	# Additional Languages
8	30%	3	5	1
9	35%	4	6	1
10-11	45%	5	7	2
12	45%	5	7	3
13-14	55%	6	9	4
15-16	65%	7	11	5
17	75%	8	14	6
18	85%	9	18	7

WISDOM

Ability Score	Magic Attack Adjustment	Spell Bonus	Chance of Spell Failure
2-3	-3	----	100%
4	-2	----	100%
5-7	-1	----	100%
8	None	----	100%
9	None	None	20%
10	None	None	15%
11	None	None	10%
12	None	None	5%
13	None	One 1st Level	0%
14	None	One 1st Level	0%
15	+1	One 2nd Level	0%
16	+2	One 2nd Level	0%
17	+3	One 3rd Level	0%
18	+4	One 4th Level	0%

DEXTERITY

Ability Score	Reaction/Attacking Adjustment	Defensive Adjustment
2-3	-3	+4
4	-2	+3
5	-1	+2
6	0	+1
7	0	0
8	0	0
9	0	0
10	0	0
11	0	0
12	0	0
13	0	0
14	0	0
15	0	-1
16	+1	-2
17	+2	-3
18	+3	-4

CONSTITUTION
Constitution is a good attribute for all classes, especially warriors.

Ability Score	Hit Point Adjustment	System Shock Survival %	Resurection Survival %
3	-2	35%	40%
4	-1	40%	45%
5	-1	45%	50%
6	-1	50%	55%
7	0	55%	60%
8	0	60%	65%
9	0	65%	70%
10	0	70%	75%
11	0	75%	80%
12	0	80%	85%
13	0	85%	90%
14	0	88%	92%
15	+1	91%	94%
16	+2	95%	96%
17	+2 (+3 for warriors)	97%	98%
18	+2 (+4 for warriors)	99%	100%

CHARISMA
Charisma is a great attribute to have if you are planning on becoming the Goblin King or making Goblin Babies.

Ability Score	Max Henchmen	Loyalty Base	Reaction Adjustment
3	1	-30%	-25%
4	1	-25%	-20%
5	2	-20%	-15%
6	2	-15%	-10%
7	3	-10%	-5%
8	3	-5%	Normal
9	4	Normal	Normal
10	4	Normal	Normal
11	4	Normal	Normal
12	5	Normal	Normal
13	5	Normal	+5%
14	6	+5%	+10%
15	7	+15%	+15%
16	8	+20%	+25%
17	10	+30%	+30%
18	15	+40%	+35%

EQUIPMENT

Adventuring Items

Backpack	2 cp	Pouch belt small	15 cp	Spike	1 cp
Chest wooden small	4 sp	Rope 25ft	4 cp	Flint steel	5 cp
Chest wooden large	8 sp	Oil flask	1 sp	Quiver bolt	15cp
Sack small	1 cp	Quiver arrow	8 cp		
Holy symbol	1 cp to 1 gp	Torch	1 cp		

Provisions

Ale - Pint	4cp	Beer pt	1cp	Mead pt	1sp
Wine good	5cp	Wine watered	2cp	Rations 1wk (mushrooms/insects)	3cp
Dried insects 1/day	1cp	Dried frogs 1/day	1cp	Rations 1 wk (rat meat)	5cp

Clothes

Belt	3cp	Boots	8cp	Cloak	1sp
Hat	1sp	Robes	6cp	Breeches	1cp
Shirt	1cp				

Armor

Animal Hide	5cp	Alligator Skin	5sp	Piece Meal Armor	1cp to 10sp
Rickety Splint Mail	50sp	Iron Wood Piece Meal	25sp	Iron Wood Plate Mail	100sp
Dented Salvagable Helm	10sp	Turtle shell shield	5sp	Dragon Scale Mail (AC -2)	GM decision
Chainmail		Leather	5cp		

Weapons

Dagger - 1D4 damage	2cp	Club - 1D6 damage	Free	Knife - 1D3 damage	1cp
Short Sword - 1D6 damage	8cp	Long Sword (2-handed) - 1D8 damage	15sp	Hammer - 1D4+1 damage	1cp
Axe - 1D6 damage	5cp	Mace - 1D6+1 damage	8cp	Spear - 1D6 damage	4cp
Dart - 1D3 damage	5cp	Short Bow	15cp	Arrow - 1D6 damage	1cp
Crossbow	50sp	Bolt - 2D6 damage	2cp		

Livestock & Mounts

Chicken	3cp	Goat	1sp	Pigeon	2cp
Piglet	1sp	Pig	3sp	Sheep	2sp
Crow	3cp	Boar	5sp	Worg	20gp
Giant Rat	25gp	Giant Spider	10gp	Giant Toad	10gp
Carrion Crawler	50gp				

Tack & Harness

Barding chain	20gp	Barding leather	5gp	Saddle	10cp
Saddle bags	4cp	Bit & bridle	15cp	Harness	1cp
Saddle blanket	3cp				

MONETARY SYSTEM

10 copper pieces (cp) = 1 silver piece
20 silver pieces (sp) = 1 gold piece
2 electrum pieces (ep) = 1 gold piece
5 gold pieces (gp) = 1 platinum piece
1 platinum piece (pp) = 5 gold pieces

Goblin Magic

Goblin magic is much different from what humans use. Goblins do not write magic spells down on scrolls or spell books. They teach spells by memory and are passed down from wizard to wizard.

Goblin wizards will hardly ever use material components in their spell casting, just verbal and semantic gestures to cast spells. Once the goblin learns a spell from another wizard, it will stay in his memory. The only item for a shaman to cast his spell is a holy symbol of his god.

A shaman also prays for new spells at midnight of any day and just picks new ones. Shamans must also make blood sacrifices on the new moon every month (creatures with souls). It's rumored that the Goblin King is a Wizard/Rogue of an unknown level.

	Goblin Wizard Spells								
	1st		2nd		3rd		4th		5th
1	Fire Fingers	1	Continual Darkness	1	Negate Magic	1	Wall of Bones	1	Cone of Frost
2	Sense Magic	2	Detect Good	2	Breath Water	2	Wall of Flames	2	Breath Fire
3	Darkness	3	Open	3	Mini-Fire Ball	3	Plant Growth	3	Screaming Wall of Fire
4	Cloud of Sleep	4	Magic Lock	4	Charm	4	Fly as Bat	4	Metamorphosis
5	Create Fog	5	Sense Invisibility	5	Fairy Tongues	5	Armor of the Goblin King	5	Create Random Magic Item
6	Fool's Gold	6	Chameleon	6	Fog of Fear	6	Fire Invulnerability		
7	See History	7	Sheet of Ice	7	Paralysis Bolt				
8	Float on Air	8	Swirling Lights						

	Goblin Shaman Spells								
	1st		2nd		3rd		4th		5th
1	Cure Damaged Monster	1	Hide Traps	1	Negate Magic	1	Cure Wounded Monster	1	Raise Monster
2	Sense Magic	2	Mask AL	2	Cause Disease	2	Mask Lie	2	Speak with God
3	Darkness	3	Track	3	Cause Blindness	3	Goblin War Banner	3	True Sight
4	Fear	4	Freeze Water	4	Curse	4	Cause Poison	4	Control Undead
5	Rot Wood	5	Charm Insect	5	Boost Undead Control	5	Armor of Meg-lubiyeti	5	Troll Regeneration
6	Dowsing	6	Float on Water/Air	6	Animate Monster	6	Create Green Slime	6	Create Pool of Magic
7	Putrefy Food & Drink	7	Goblin War Drums	7	Call Monster				
8	Create Alter	8	Boost Prime Attribute						

WIZARD 1ST LEVEL SPELLS

Fire Fingers

Level: 1
Range: 0
Duration: 1 round
Area of Effect: Special

Components: V, S
Casting Time: 1 segment
Saving Throw: None

Description: When the wizard casts this spell, jets of searing flame shoot from his fingertips; the Fire Fingers send out flame jets of 2' length in a horizontal arc of about 80° in front of the wizard. Any creature in the area of flames takes 1 hit point of damage for each level of experience of the spell caster, and no Saving Throw is possible. Inflammable materials touched by the fire will burn, i.e. cloth, paper, parchment, thin wood, etc.

Sense Magic
Level: 1
Range: 0
Duration: 2 rounds/level
Area of Effect: 1″ path, 3″ long
Components: V
Casting Time: 1 segment
Saving Throw: None

Description: When the sense magic spell is cast, the wizard detects magical radiations in a path 1″ wide, and up to 3″ long, in the direction, he or she is facing. The caster can turn 60° per round.

Darkness
Level: 1
Range: 1″/level
Duration: 1 turn/level
Area of Effect: 2″ radius globe
Components: V, S
Casting Time: 2 segments
Saving Throw: None

Description: This spell causes a 2″ radius globe of natural darkness. Normal lights only function at a fraction of what they would typically emit. Magic light spells negate the effect of this spell. Rogues gain a +30% to hide skills while in this darkness.

Cloud of Sleep
Level: 1
Range: 3″ +1″/level
Duration: 2 rounds/level
Area of Effect: 2″x2″x2″
Components: V, S
Casting Time: 1 segment
Saving Throw: Neg.

Description: When a wizard casts a Cloud of Sleep spell, it will usually affect every creature in the area (other than undead and particular other creatures specifically excluded from the spell's effects). All creatures to be affected must be within a 2″ diameter circle that may move at 1″ a round. All affected will sleep until the cloud dissipates. The cloud of sleep will only effect creatures up to 4 HD. All creatures effected get a + 1 per hit dice to resist the sleep effects, so a 4 HD creature would get a + 4 to saving throws.

Create Fog
Level: 1
Range: 12″
Duration: 1 turn/level
Area of Effect: 2″ / level
Components: V, S
Casting Time: 1 round
Saving Throw: None

Description: The wizard creates a 2″ fog per level of the caster. This will obscure the vision of most creatures giving blind modifiers to the enemy. The wizard is not affected by the fog, nor is his allies if so desired.

Fool's Gold
Level: 1
Range: 1″
Duration: 5 turns /level
Area of Effect: 1 cubic ft per level of wizard
Components: S
Casting Time: 1 round
Saving Throw: Neg.

Description: The wizard to cause any object (up to 2000gp in weight per level of caster) to appear to be made of gold. The effect will remain till the duration of the spell is up. Those who save will see through the illusion and see the true image of the object.

See History of Magic Item

Level: 1
Range: 0
Duration: 1 segment /level
Area of Effect: 1 Item
Components: V, S
Casting Time: 1 turn
Saving Throw: Special

Description: When the See History of Magic Item spell is cast, one item may be touched and handled by the wizard so that he may possibly find what magic it possesses. The wizard sees the past history of the magic item. Seeing the past wielders of the item, how it was used, and what effects it might have caused.

The item in question must be held or worn as would be expected for any such object, i.e., a bracelet must be placed on the spell caster's wrist, a helm on his or her head, boots on the feet, a cloak worn, a dagger held, and so on. Note that any consequences of this use of the item falls entirely upon the wizard, although any saving throw normally allowed is still the privilege of the wizard. For each segment the spell is in force, it is 15% + 5% per level of the wizard probable that 1 property of the object touched can become known — possibly that the item has no properties. When a property can be known, the GM will secretly roll to see if the wizard made his saving throw versus magic. If the save was successful, the property is known; if it is 1 point short, a false power will be revealed; and if it is lower than 1 under the required score, no information will be gained.

Float on Air

Level: 1
Range: 1' /level
Duration: 1 round /level
Area of Effect: 1 target
Components: V
Casting Time: 1 /10 segment
Saving Throw: None

Description: When this spell is cast, the wizard can float on air as if like a leaf or feather. It can be used to slow the wizard's rate from a fall or used to float on top of the water. Movement is quite slow while floating in the air 1/8 th normal speed half attacks and no DEX modifier to AC.

WIZARD 2ND LEVEL SPELLS

Continual Darkness

Level: 2
Range: 1"/level
Duration: permanent
Area of Effect: 2" radius globe
Components: V, S
Casting Time: 5 segments
Saving Throw: None

Description: This spell causes a 2" radius globe of natural darkness. Normal lights only function at a fraction of the light they would typically emit. Magic light spells negate the effect of this spell. Rogues gain a +30% to Hide skills while in this darkness.

Detect Good

Level: 2
Range: 3"
Duration: 4 rounds/level
Area of Effect: 6" long
Components: V, S
Casting Time: 2 segments
Saving Throw: None

Description: This spell will indicate to the wizard whether any person, creature object or place within a 30' ft radius is good.

Open

Level: 2
Range: 5"
Duration: Special
Area of Effect: 8ft sq/level
Components: V
Casting Time: 1 segment
Saving Throw: None

Description: The open spell will open stuck, held, or magic locked doors. It will also open barred or otherwise locked doors. It causes secret doors to open. The open spell will also open locked or trick-opening boxes or chests. It will loosen shackles or chains as well. If it is used to open a magic locked door, the open spell does not remove the former spell, but it simply suspends its functioning for 1 turn. In all other cases, the open will permanently open locks or welds — although the former could be closed and locked again after that. It will not raise bars or similar impediments (such as a portcullis).

Magic Lock

Level: 2
Range: Touch
Duration: permanent
Area of Effect: 20 sq ft/level
Components: V, S
Casting Time: 2 segments
Saving Throw: None

Description: When a magic lock spell is cast upon a door, chest, or portal, it magically locks it. The magic-locked door or object can be opened only by breaking, a dispel or negate magic, an open spell, or by a wizard 4 or more levels higher than the one casting the spell. Note that the last two methods do not remove the magic lock. They only negate it for a brief duration.

Sense Invisibility

Level: 2
Range: 1"/level
Duration: 2 rounds/level
Area of Effect: 1" path
Components: V, S
Casting Time: 1 segment
Saving Throw: None

Description: The spell allows the recipient to see any invisible objects or being as well as astral, ethereal, hidden, invisible or out-of-phase creatures.

Chameleon

Level: 2
Range: touch
Duration: 1 turn/level
Area of Effect: self or touched
Components: V, S
Casting Time: 1 segment
Saving Throw: None

Description: This spell allows the affected person or object to alter the color and pattern of his clothes, armor, and physical body. Allowing to blend into the surroundings. The recipient must remain completely still for the effect to function correctly.

Sheet of Ice

Level: 2
Range: 5"
Duration: 5 rounds/level
Area of Effect: 1" radius
Components: V, S, M
Casting Time: 5 segments
Saving Throw: ½ movement

Description: This spell creates a sheet of ice coating any objects or the ground with two inches of ice, making it very slick and slippery save vs. spell for half movement Otherwise slowed to a stop or fallen, critical fail is rolled. If cast on an object or Objects, save to maintain a Grip or hold. The material components of this spell is copper wire.

Swirling Lights
Level: 2
Range: 1″
Duration: 5 rounds/level
Area of Effect: 2″ radius
Components: V
Casting Time: 3 segments
Saving Throw: Neg.

Description: The wizard creates a swirling mass of lights which causes a hypnotic pattern causing one individual around to save vs. spell or have a suggestion implanted into ones psyche, the person will respond only to simple suggestions and cannot be forced to do something against his nature.

WIZARD 3ʳᴰ LEVEL SPELLS

Negate Magic
Level: 3
Range: 5″
Duration: permanent
Area of Effect: 2.5″ cube
Components: V, S
Casting Time: 6 segments
Saving Throw: None

Description: Negate Magic removes spells cast upon persons or objects or counter the casting of spells in the area of effect. The base chance for success of a dispel magic spell is 50%. For every level of experience of the character casting the dispel magic above that of the creature whose magic is to be dispelled (or above the efficiency level of the object from which the magic is issuing), the base chance increases by 5%, so that if there are 10 levels of difference, there is a 100% chance. For every level below the experience/efficiency level of the creature/object, the base chance is reduced by 2%.

Breath Water
Level: 3
Range: Touch
Duration: 5 turns/level
Area of Effect: Creature Touched
Components: V, S, M
Casting Time: 5 segments
Saving Throw: None

Description: The recipient of a breath water spell can freely breathe underwater for the duration of the spell, i.e., 5 turns for each level of the wizard casting the spell. The material components of this spell are a fish scale and a glass bottle.

Mini-Fire Ball
Level: 3
Range: 5″ + 1″/level
Duration: Instantaneous
Area of Effect: per target
Components: V, S, M
Casting Time: 1 segment
Saving Throw: 1/2

Description: When cast, the Mini-fireball cause 1 sphere for each level of the caster to appear and instantly strike its target. Each one causes 1D4 per level of the caster. Multiple Spheres may strike the same target with a save for each. Besides causing damage to creatures, the mini fireball(s) ignite all combustible materials within its area, and the heat will melt soft metals such as gold, copper, silver, etc. Items exposed to the spell's effects must be rolled to determine if they are affected.

Items with a creature that makes its saving throw are considered unaffected. The wizard points his finger and speaks the targets at which the mini fireball(s) is to burst. A streak flashes from the pointing digit and flowers into the mini fireball(s). If creatures fail their saving throws; they take full hit-point damage from the blast. Those who make saving throws manage to dodge, fall flat, or roll aside, taking ½ the full hit point damage. The material component of this spell is a firefly.

Charm

Level: 3
Range: 7"
Duration: 5 rounds/level
Area of Effect: 1 creature
Components: V, S, M
Casting Time: 1 segment
Saving Throw: Neg.

Description: This spell affects1 intelligent creature. The spell does not enable the wizard to control the charmed creature as if it were an automaton, but any word or action of the wizard will be viewed in its most favorable way. Thus, a charmed creature would not obey a suicide command but might believe the wizard if assured that the only chance to save the wizard's life is if the creature holds back an onrushing paladin for "just a round or two". Note also that the spell does not empower the wizard with linguistic capabilities beyond those he normally possesses. The material components of this spell is honeycomb

Fairy Tongues

Level: 3
Range: self /Other
Duration: 1 Turn/level
Area of Effect: 1 creature
Components: V
Casting Time: 3 segments
Saving Throw: None

Description: This spell enables the caster to speak read write and understand all languages.

Fog of Fear

Level: 3
Range: 6"
Duration: 4 rounds/level
Area of Effect: 3" radius
Components: V, S
Casting Time: 4 segments
Saving Throw: Neg.

Description: This fog has swirling forms of monsters and ethereal creatures. All in its radius must make a successful saving throw or flee for 1d6 rounds. They cannot attack anything and lose all dexterity modifiers.

Paralysis Bolt

Level: 3
Range: 8"
Duration: 3 rounds/level
Area of Effect: 1 creature
Components: S
Casting Time: 3 segments
Saving Throw: Neg.

Description: This magic energy bolt renders the victim paralyzed for 3 rounds per level of the wizard, unless a saving throw is successful. The Paralysis Bolt will not work on the undead.

WIZARD 4TH LEVEL SPELLS

Wall of Bones

Level: 4
Range: 8"
Duration: 1 Turn/level
Area of Effect: 1"x1"x"1 / level
Components: V, S, M
Casting Time: 6 segments
Saving Throw: Special

Description: This spell manifests a wall of bones to spring forth from the ground. Passing through a Wall of Bone will take a full round and cause 1d8 to small or large creature if a saving throw is made. If failed, D8 per round, and the creature will be trapped until success is made. Large creatures cannot pass through a wall of bones but may break through it by causing 20 hp per 1" cube area to destroy while taking 1d8 damage a round if save is failed. The material components of this spell human bones.

Wall of Flames
Level: 4
Range: 7"
Duration: 2 rounds/level
Area of Effect: 1"x 1"x1" /level
Components: V, S, M
Casting Time: 1 segment
Saving Throw: 1/2

Description: The wall of flames brings forth a blazing wall of reds, yellows, and oranges causing 2d8 damage per 1" of volume if passing through the wall and igniting all flammable objects an items. On the individual, even magic items need to save vs magic fire or be destroyed. The material components of this spell are amber and a silver mirror.

Plant Growth
Level: 4
Range: 12"
Duration: Permanent
Area of Effect: 2" × 2" square area/level
Components: V, S
Casting Time: 1 round
Saving Throw: None

Description: When the wizard casts a plant growth spell, he or she causes normal vegetation to grow, entwine, and entangle. Creatures must hack or force a way through it at a movement rate of 1" per or 2" per with respect to larger-than-man-sized creatures.

Fly as Bat
Level: 4
Range: Touch
Duration: 1 ½ Turns/level
Area of Effect: Creature Touched
Components: V, S
Casting Time: 3 segments
Saving Throw: None

Description: This spell enables the wizard to bestow the power of magical flight, but the caster must flap their arms as if he was a bat. The creature affected can move vertically and/or horizontally at a rate of 12" per move (half that if ascending, twice that if descending in a dive). The exact duration of the spell is always unknown to the spell caster.

Armor of the Goblin King
Level: 4
Range: Touch
Duration: 2 Turns/level
Area of Effect: Creature Touched
Components: V, S, M
Casting Time: 2 segments
Saving Throw: None

Description: When the wizard casts this spell, a shimmering suit of plate mail appears on the wizard or creature touched AC 2 with no encumbrances or weight. The caster may move and cast spells as if not wearing armor. The material component of this spell is human babies teeth.

Fire Invulnerability

Level: 4
Range: Touch
Duration: Special
Area of Effect: Creature Touch
Components: V, S, M
Casting Time: 4 segments
Saving Throw: None

Description: When this spell is cast upon the wizard, it confers complete invulnerability to normal fires (torches, bonfires, oil fires, and the like) and to exposure to magical fires such as demon fire, burning hands, fiery dragon breath, fire ball, fire seeds, firestorm, flame strike, hell hound breath, meteor swarm, pyro hydra breath, etc., until an accumulation of 10 hit points of potential damage per level of experience of the wizard has been absorbed by the fire invulnerability spell, at which time the spell is negated. Otherwise, the spell lasts for 1 turn per level of experience of the wizard. If the spell is cast upon another creature, it gives invulnerability to normal fire gives a bonus of +4 on saving throw die rolls made versus fire attacks, and reduces damage sustained from magical fires by 60%. The material components of this spell is Hellgrammite.

WIZARD 5TH LEVEL SPELLS

Cone of Frost

Level: 5
Range: 0
Duration: Instantaneous
Area of Effect: Special
Components: V, S, M
Casting Time: 5 segments
Saving Throw: ½

Description: When this spell is cast, it causes a cone-shaped area originating at the wizard's hand in a cone 1" long per level of the caster. It drains heat energy and causes 1 four-sided die, hit point of damage (1d4), per level of experience of the wizard. For example, a 10th-level wizard would cast a cone of cold, causing 10d4 hit points of damage. The material component of this spell is a silver coin.

Breath Fire

Level: 5
Range: 0
Duration: 2 rounds/level
Area of Effect: 1" path per level
Components: V, S, M
Casting Time: 3 segments
Saving Throw: None

Explanation/Description: When this spell is cast, it causes a cone-shaped area originating at the wizard's mouth and extending outwards in a cone 1" path per level of the caster causing 1D6 hit points in damage per level of caster. The material component of this spell is a scarab beetle.

Screaming Wall of Fire

Level: 5
Range: 8"
Duration: 2 rounds/level
Area of Effect: 1" x 1"x1"
Components: V, S, M
Casting Time: 2 segments
Saving Throw: ½

Description: When this spell is cast, flames bring forth a blazing wall of reds, yellows, and oranges, causing 2d8 damage per 1" of volume if passing through the wall and igniting all flammable objects and items. On the individual, even magic items need to save vs. magic fire or be destroyed. Also, anyone gazing upon the screaming wall of fire must save vs. spell or disengage for 1d6 rounds if no exit
route is available and will curl up in the fetal position for the same amount of time. The material components of this spell are Pumpkin Seeds.

Metamorphosis

Level: 5
Range: Touch
Duration: 2 Turns/level
Area of Effect: Creature Touched
Components: V, S, M
Casting Time: 4 segments
Saving Throw: None

Description: When this spell is cast, the wizard can assume the form of any creature — from as small as a mouse to as large as a dragon — and its way of moving as well. For example, if you became a green slime, you could slither under doors or gain flight as a dragon. The spell does not give the other abilities (attack, magic, etc.), nor does it run the risk of changing personality and mentality. No "system shock" check is required. Thus, a wizard changed to a raven could fly, but his vision would be of a goblin. A change to an ochre jelly would enable movement under doors or along halls and ceilings but not the jelly's offensive or defensive capabilities. Naturally, the strength of the new form must be sufficient to allow normal movement. The spell caster can change his form as often as desired, the change requiring only 6 segments. Damage to the metamorphic form is computed as if it was inflicted upon the wizard, but when the wizard returns to his or her own form, from 1 to 10 (d10), points of damage are restored. The material component of this spell is a gold coin

Create Random Magic Item

Level: 5
Range: 0
Duration: Permanent
Area of Effect: 1 Item
Components: V, S, M
Casting Time: 12 Hours
Saving Throw: None

Description: When this spell is cast depending on the item being enchanted will determine its type whatever item is being used, has to be of exceptional quality. Also, having a sacrifice. Some part of the wizard casting the spell, a finger, a toe, or even an eyeball or possibly an ear hair will not suffice. After casting this spell, the wizard will lose one permanent Con point and must rest for 24 hours. The magic item will be rolled on Random Magic Item Chart on page 32 or up to the Game master's discretion. The material component of this spell is human blood.

SHAMAN 1ST LEVEL SPELLS

Cure Damaged Monster

Level: 1
Range: Touch
Duration: Permanent
Area of Effect: Being Touched
Components: V, S
Casting Time: 5 segments
Saving Throw: None

Description: Upon laying his or her hand upon a creature, the shaman cures 1D8 +1 hit points of wounds or other injury damage to the creature's body to be healed. Note that cured wounds are permanent only insofar as the creature does not sustain further damage, and that caused wounds will heal just as any normal injury will.

Sense Magic

Level: 1
Range: 0
Duration: 2 rounds/level
Area of Effect: 1" path, 3" long
Components: V
Casting Time: 1 segment
Saving Throw: None

Description: When the Sense Magic spell is cast, the wizard detects magical radiations in a path 1" wide, and up to 3" long, in the direction, he or she is facing. The caster can turn 60° per round.

Darkness
Level: 1
Range: 1"/level
Duration: 1 turn/level
Area of Effect: 2" radius globe
Components: V, S
Casting Time: 2 segments
Saving Throw: None

Description: This spell causes a 2" radius globe of natural darkness. Normal lights only function at a fraction of the light they would normally emit. Magic light spells negate the effect of this spell. Rogues gain a +30% to hide skills while in this darkness.

Fear
Level: 1
Range: 0
Duration: 1 round/level
Area of Effect: 1" path, 6" long
Components: V, S, M
Casting Time: 3 segments
Saving Throw: Neg.

Description: When a Fear Spell is cast, the shaman sends forth an invisible ray that causes creatures within its area of effect to turn away from the spell caster and flee in panic. Affected creatures are likely to drop whatever they are holding when struck by the spell. Save vs. Dex to maintain holding their items. The material component of this spell is a glass eye.

Rot Wood
Level: 1
Range: 3"
Duration: Permanent
Area of Effect: 10Lbs / level
Components: V, S
Casting Time: 5 segments
Saving Throw: Neg.

Description: This spell, when cast rots wood 10 lbs. per level of the caster. If the wood affected fails its save, affected wood will become brittle and useless.

Dowsing
Level: 1
Range: 10"radius
Duration: 5 rounds/level
Area of Effect: special
Component: V, S, M
Casting Time: 1 round
Saving Throw: None

Description: This spell allows the shaman to sense the location of all semi-large sources of water in any direction, even through rock or walls. The material component of this spell is a wood stick forked at the end.

Putrefy Food & Drink
Level: 1
Range: 2"
Duration: Permanent
Area of Effect: 1" cubic ft/level 1" sq
Component: V, S
Casting Time: 1 round
Saving Throw: None

Description: When cast, the spell will spoil, rot, or otherwise contaminate food and/or water, whereby only a goblin or animal can handle such foul food and drink. Up to 1 cubic foot of food and/or drink can be thus made suitable for consumption by goblins and alike. This spell will even spoil holy water.

Create Altar

Level: 1
Range: 3"
Duration: Special
Area of Effect: 3" radius
Component: V, S, M
Casting Time: 1 Turn
Saving Throw: None

Description: When cast by the shaman, this spell creates a sinister looking altar made of wooden shapes and designs dating back 1000s of goblin years. The altar is immobile unless the shaman makes special preparations by building a platform ahead of time, having at least 10 goblins available to carry the altar. The altar is semi-permanent unless it 20 hp of damage in which it is destroyed. While active, it bestows all attacks, damage, and saving throws made by those in the area of effect who are friendly to the shaman and are at +1, while those of the shaman's enemies are at -1. Also, if the shaman prays at this magic altar when recovering spells, he will be granted 1 extra first-level spell that day. The material components of this spell are whole human organs pierced with the wood of the altar.

SHAMAN 2ND LEVEL SPELLS

Hide Traps

Level: 2
Range: 4"
Duration: 1 turn/level
Area of Effect: 3" radius
Components: V, S
Casting Time: 4 segments
Saving Throw: Special

Description: This spell, when cast, masks all traps by a magical nature, not allowing normal thieving detection unless aided by magical means. If a magic detection source is used, the caster must make a save vs. magic for their spell to function correctly. Otherwise, they are deluded by the trap's presence.

Mask Alignment

Level: 2
Range: 1"
Duration: 1 turn/level
Area of Effect: up to 10 creatures
Components: V, S
Casting Time: 1 round
Saving Throw: None

Description: This spell masks the aura of a creature and totally obscures the alignment, into changing the aura to any alignment, one shift from its normal. A neutral could pose as a good or evil as a neutral.

Track

Level: 2
Range: touch
Duration: 1 turn /level
Area of Effect: creature touched.
Components: V, S, M
Casting Time: 1 round
Saving Throw: None

Description: When this spell is cast, the recipient can track a known creature if having a piece of its possession, i.e., a scrap of cloth or an object handled recently. Having a 90% chance of tracking its subject even across water or through secret doors much like a bloodhound. The material component of this spell is a rabbit's foot.

Freeze Water
Level: 2
Range: 3"
Duration: 2 special
Area of Effect: Special
Components: V, S
Casting Time: 1 round
Saving Throw: None

Description: When this spell is cast, the shaman can freeze 25 gallons of water or liquid per level. The liquid will remain frozen until it melts due to normal means.

Charm Insect
Level: 2
Range: 3"
Duration: 2 rounds/level
Area of Effect: line of sight
Components: V, S
Casting Time: 4 segments
Saving Throw: None

Description: When this spell is cast, it will charm all insects in the shaman's view. This spell is handy while having giant insects in the view of the caster. No save.

Float on Water/Air
Level: 2
Range: Touch
Duration: 1 round /level
Area of Effect: creature touched.
Components: V, S
Casting Time: 1 segment
Saving Throw: None

Description: When this spell is cast, the shaman becomes weightless, allowing the shaman to float on water or float down a pit. Movement is halved while moving across water.

Goblin War Drums
Level: 2
Range: Self
Duration: special
Area of Effect: Ear shot
Components: V, S, M
Casting Time: 5 segments
Saving Throw: None

Description: When this spell is cast, the shaman will begin playing a set of drums. The spell's duration will be as long as the shaman plays uninterrupted. All allies within hearing of the drumming will gain +1hit /+1 dam +1 hp +1 AC + 2 morale checks and immune to all forms of Fear spells and abilities. Does not stack. The material component of this spell is a small drum covered in human skins.

Boost Prime Attribute
Level: 2
Range: touch
Duration: 2 rounds/level
Area of Effect: creature touched.
Components: V, S, M
Casting Time: 5 segments
Saving Throw: None

Description: When the shaman casts this spell, it will boost whatever the prime attribute of the creature, the main class would be by 1d6 points. All modifiers will last until the boost is over. The material component of this spell is Unholy Water.

SHAMAN 3RD LEVEL SPELLS

Negate Magic
Level: 3
Range: 5"
Duration: permanent
Area of Effect: 2.5" cube
Components: V, S
Casting Time: 6 segments
Saving Throw: None

Description: Negate Magic removes spells cast upon persons or objects or counters the casting of spells in the area of effect. The base chance for success of a Negate Magic spell is 50%. For every level of experience of the character casting the Negate Magic above that of the creature whose magic is to be negated (or above the efficiency level of the object from which the magic is issuing), the base chance increases by 5%, so that if there are 10 levels of difference, there is a 100% chance. For every level below the experience/efficiency level of the creature/object, the base chance is reduced by 2%.

Cause Disease
Level: 3
Range: Touch
Duration: permanent
Area of Effect: Creature touched.
Components: V, S
Casting Time: 1 round
Saving Throw: Neg.

Description: When this spell is cast upon a creature, the disease caused will begin to affect the victim in 1-6 turns, causing the afflicted creature to lose 1 hit point per turn, and 1 point of strength per hour until the creature is at 5% of the original hit points and strength.

Cause Blindness
Level: 3
Range: Touch
Duration: Permanent
Area of Effect: Creature touched.
Components: V, S
Casting Time: 1 round
Saving Throw: Neg.

Description: When this spell has been cast the target must save vs. spell or be blinded suffering all ill effects of blindness until death or cured. There is now -4 to hit and no DEX bonus.

Curse
Level: 3
Range: touch
Duration: Special
Area of Effect: Person or object
Components: V, S
Casting Time: 5 segments
Saving Throw: Neg.

Description: When the shaman casts this spell on a creature, it must save vs. magic or be cursed for 1/day per level of the shaman. The curse is maybe as simple as -4 on all to-hit rolls or -4 on all saving throws or as complex as the GM wants to allow. If cast on an object, no save and a curse is permanent until the item is dispelled or destroyed.

Boost Undead Control
Level: 3
Range: touch
Duration: 2 rounds/level
Area of Effect: self or touch
Components: V, S
Casting Time: 1 segment
Saving Throw: None

Description: When the shaman casts this spell, he increases the success of undead control by +3 and doubles the numbers befriended.

Animate Monster

Level: 3
Range: 1"
Duration: Permanent
Area of Effect: Special
Components: V, S, M
Casting Time: 1 round
Saving Throw: None

Description: When the shaman casts this spell, he may animate any dead creature as a zombie or a skeleton. It will have no special attacks of its original life except 3/4 its original hit points. The spell will animate the monsters until they are destroyed or until the magic is dispelled. The shaman may animate 1 creature per level he has attended. The material component of this spell is a drop of unicorn blood.

Call Monster

Level: 3
Range: 3"
Duration: 3 rounds+1/level
Area of Effect: Special
Components: V, S
Casting Time: 4 segments
Saving Throw: None

Description: When the shaman casts this spell, he calls 1-6 monsters within a 1 mile distance to instantly appear at the spot the shaman desired. They will attack the spell user's opponents to the best of their ability until they are commanded to cease, the spell duration expires, or the monsters are slain. Note that if no opponent exists to fight, summoned monsters can, if communication is possible and if they are physically capable, perform other services for the summoning shaman.

SHAMAN 4TH LEVEL SPELLS

Cure Wounded Monster

Level: 4
Range: Touch
Duration: Permanent
Area of Effect: Monster touched
Components: V, S
Casting Time: 7 segments
Saving Throw: None

Description: This spell is a more potent version of the Cure Damaged Monster spell. Upon laying his hand upon a creature, the shaman cures 3 to 17 (2d8 + 1) hit points of damage.

Mask Lie

Level: 4
Range: Self/ Other
Duration: 1 turn/level
Area of Effect: Creature Touched
Components: V, S
Casting Time: 5 segments
Saving Throw: None

Description: This spell masks the creature from all forms of detection, including detect alignments and auras. This powerful spell can even fool True Sight.

Goblin War Banner

Level: 4
Range: Self
Duration: 2 turns/level
Area of Effect: 100 ft radius
Components: V, S, M
Casting Time: 1 round
Saving Throw: None

Description: While the goblin waves this banner, no goblin in the area effect will break and run from a morale check. They also gain +1 on all saves, and get a +1 bonus on hit and damage. The material component of this spell is ink.

Cause Poison

Level: 4
Range: Touch
Duration: 1 round/level
Area of Effect: 1 creature
Components: V, S
Casting Time: 1 segment
Saving Throw: Neg.

Description: The shaman may choose an effect of poison if save is missed, paralyzation, sleep, or death. The shaman must make a successful hit to cast spell. Only 3 attempts to hit can be made, otherwise, the spell is lost for the day.

Armor of Meg-lubiyeti

Level: 4
Range: Self / Other
Duration: 1 Turn/level
Area of Effect: creature touched.
Components: V, S, M
Casting Time: 1 round
Saving Throw: None

When the shaman cast this spell, shimmering armor appears on the target. This gives the creature AC 0 for the duration of the spell and immunity to normal weapons. They now require a +2 or better weapon to hit the wearer of the armor. The material component of this spell is a drop of a dragons blood.

Create Green Slime

Level: 4
Range: 3"
Duration: Permanent
Area of Effect: Special
Components: V, S, M
Casting Time: 1 Turn
Saving Throw: None

Description: I bet you always wondered where green slime came from. When the shaman casts this spell, he creates a green slime of 1 cubic ft per level. This spell does not allow to control or command the green slime. Once created, it will attack anything. The material component of this spell is phlegm and meal worms.

SHAMAN 5TH LEVEL SPELLS

Raise Monster
Level: 5
Range: 3"
Duration: Permanent
Area of Effect: 1 creature
Components: V, S
Casting Time: 1 round
Saving Throw: Special

Description: When the shaman casts a Raise Monster spell, he can restore life to 1 creature. The length of time in which the creature has been dead is of importance, as the shaman can raise the monster only up to a certain point. The limit is 1 day for each level of experience of the shaman, i.e., a 9th-level shaman can raise a creature dead for up to 9 days. Note that the creature's body must be whole, or otherwise, missing parts will still be missing when the creature is brought back to life. Also, the resurrected creature must make a special saving throw to survive the ordeal. The somatic component of the spell is a pointed finger.

Speak with God
Level: 5
Range: Self
Duration: 1 round /level
Area of Effect: Self
Components: V, S, M
Casting Time: 1 round
Saving Throw: Special

Description: The shaman goes into a trance, allowing him to ask 1 question a round to his god. The god may answer however it chooses at the end of the spell. The shaman must make a save vs. magic or suffer whatever the god's will is, will it be a quest, death, alignment change, or even a sex change? As the GM be creative. The material component of this spell is a wisp of smoke.

True Sight
Level: 5
Range: touch
Duration: 1 round/level
Area of Effect: 10" view
Components: V, S
Casting Time: 7 segments
Saving Throw: None

Description: When the shaman employs this spell, all things within the area of the True Sight effect appear as they are. Secret doors become plain. The exact location of displaced things is obvious. Invisible things and those which are astral or ethereal become quite visible. Illusions and apparitions are seen through. Polymorphed, changed or magicked things are apparent. Even the aura projected by creatures becomes visible so that the shaman is able to know whether they are good, evil, or in between.

Control Undead
Level: 5
Range: 8"
Duration: 1 turn/level
Area of Effect: 6" diameter circle
Components: V, S
Casting Time: 7 segments
Saving Throw: Negate

Description: When this spell is cast, all undead must save vs. magic or be under the total control of the shaman until the duration of the spell is up.

Troll Regeneration

Level: 5
Range: Touch
Duration: 2 rounds/level
Area of Effect: 1 creature
Components: V, S
Casting Time: 5 segments
Saving Throw: None

Description: When the Shaman casts this spell, he regenerates as if he were a troll. He recovers 3 HP a round and includes the rebounding of severed members. The only disadvantage is that if burnt fire while this spell is active, it will cancel the spell.

Create Pool of Magic

Level: 5
Range: 1"
Duration: permanent
Area of Effect: Special
Components: V, S, M
Casting Time: Special
Saving Throw: None

Description: This very powerful spell is how magic pools are born by the shaman. You may only cast this spell on a full moon with the help of many goblins, depending on the size of the magic pool you want to fill. This magic pool may have many different effects and types depending on the GM's choices. Here is one idea, but all effects are solely up to the GM. Roll 1D6 1-3 neg effect, 4-6 positive effect, roll 1D6 to effect ability score plus or minus 1D6 depending on effects. However, many goblins need to fill the area wanting to use it with urine. That's right! All you humans have been drinking goblin urine for 50 years! The material component of this spell is goblin urine.

RANDOM MAGIC ITEMS

To determine item use D100 & D6 to roll 1-200. 1-3 on d6 =1-100. 4-6 = 101-200, then roll 2 D10s.

Potions		1 dose=D6 + 6 turns
01-05	Delusion	Imbiber believes a differnt potion has taken effect determine type randomly.
06-10	Diminution	Shrink to 6 inches, less for a partial dose.
11-15	Flying	Fly 120 feet per turn.
16-20	Gaseous Form	Imbiber, but not gear, turns to gas, control is retained.
21-25	Long Life	Reduces goblins game age 2-12 years.
26-30	Growth	Grow to 30 feet, less for a partial dose.
30-35	Haste	Move at twice normal speed and get two attacks per round.
36-40	Healing	Heal 1d6+1.
41-45	Invisibility	Turn invisible for duration, unless an attack is made.
46-50	Poison	Save vs. poison or die.

Rings		Only 1 or 2 can be worn at one time.
51	Contrariness	Wearer does the opposite of normal or what is requested.
52	Control Animals	While concentrating, can control 3D6 small, 2D6 medium, or 1D6 large animals.
53	Control Plants	While concentrating, can control 1-6 large or 10' of plants or fungi.
54	Fire Resistance	Immunity to normal fire; +2 save vs. breath and -1 damage per die
55	Invisibility	Turn invisible until an attack is made.
56	Protection +1	Gain -1 AC, +1 on all saves
57	Regeneration	Heal 1 hit point per turn unless damaged by fire or acid.
58	Water Walking	Walk on any liquid.
59	Weakness	Lose 10% of STR/turn until at 1/2; 1 in 20 cause reverse, up to 18 max.
60	Asanal's Wonderous Ring	The first time you fail a save against a curse or other magic, the ring breaks and you instead make your save.

Rods/Staves/Wands		Wands can only be used by Wizards and have D100 charges remaining.
61	Rod of Slaying Humans	When a successful hit is made on a human save vs. death magic or die!
62	Rod of the Goblin King	All creatures within 2˝ radius to be charmed (no save) 1 charge a turn +2 Mace otherwise.
63	Staff of the Snake	Shaman only, +1 to hit, 1D6+1 damage, can coil around target for 1D4 turns.
64	Staff of Healing	Shaman only, heals 1D6+1, usable once per day per character.
65	Wand of Cold	60´ x 30´ cone, 6D6 damage, save vs. breath for 1/2.
66	Wand of Detect Magic	All magic items in a 20´ range glow.
67	Wand of Detect Secret Door	Points to all secret doors and traps in a 20´ range.
68	Wand of Fear	60´ x 30´ cone; save vs. wands or flee for 1D3 turns, drop all held items.
69	Wand of Fire Balls	240´ range, 20´ radius, 6D6 damage, save vs. breath for 1/2
70	Wand of Paralyzation	60´ x 30´ cone, save vs. wands or be paralyzed for 6 turns.

Misc.		
71-82	Asanal's Mystical Key	A key that can unlock any door, but cannot be removed from the mechanism until the door is relocked.
83-86	Armor of the E.G.G.	Looks like a fancy dinner suit. Is actually a suit of plate mail.
87-98	Whistle of the Duck	This is a magical duck shaped whistle. When blown, roll for a random encounter.
99-110	Goblin Cloak	Invisible while in shadowy areas, but has a horrific odor +2 CHA checks to goblinoids.

Various		
111	Bag of Holding	Holds 10,000 coins as 300; or object 10´ x 5´ x 3´ as 600 coins.
112	Bag of Destroying	Appears to be a Bag of Holding but eats contents in D6+6 turns.
113	Broom of Flying	Fly at 240 feet/turn or 180 feet/turn with passenger, command word activates.
114	Crystal Ball	Wizard only, can see images at distance three times per day.
115	ESP Medallion	Wearer can read thoughts up to 60´, fails 1 in 6, foiled by lead or over 2´ rock.
116	Hydra Teeth 1D10	Once planted in the ground, would grow into fully grown skeleton warriors AC5 HP10 Dam1D8
117	Gauntlets of Ogre Power	Adds 2-8 points of damage per blow, carry 1000 extra coins.
118	Helm of Telepathy	Read & suggest thoughts in 90´, unless save vs. spells at -1, -2 for resistance.
119	Helm of Evil/Good	Changes wearer to opposite alignment, neutral stays neutral.
120	Rope of Climbing	50´ long, holds 10,000 coins in weight, obeys commands to climb up or down.

Weapons/Armor					
121-124	Armor +1	149-152	Sword +1	173-176	Sword +1, Locate Object as per spell
125-128	Armor -2	153-156	Sword +2	177-180	Sword +1, +2 vs. MUs/Enchanted
129-132	Shield +1	157-160	Sword +3	181-184	Sword +1, +2 vs. Regenerating, +3 vs. Undead
133-136	Arrows +1, 1d20	161-164	Sword -1	185-187	Sword +2, +3 vs. Thieves, Assassins, & Acrobats
137-140	Bow +1	165-168	Sword -2	188-192	Sword +2, +3 vs. Dwarves, Gnomes, & Halflings
141-144	Axe +1	169-171	Hammer +1	193-196	Dagger +1 vs. Mansize beings +2 Large beings
145-148	Spear +1	172	Hammer +2	197-200	Dagger +2 vs. Female beings +3 vs. Male beings

Cursed items require a Remove Curse spell to be cast on the wielder before the item can be discarded.

ENCOUNTER CHART

#	Encounter	DXT	HD (D8)	AC	MV	Special	AL	TD	TT	APP
1	Giant Rat	1d3	1/2	7	120	5% disease / Fears fire	N	Rubbish, scavengers	C	1-8
2	Hobgoblin	1D8	1+1	6	90	Fear Save+1 / Lead equal to ogres	LE	Strong morale	D	2-5
3	Stirge	1d3	1	7	180	Attacks at +2 hit / Drains -D4hp/round	N	Flying bloodsucker	Q	1-12
4	Lizardman	1D8	2+1	5	60	Swim 2x MV / ATT spears/clubs	N	Aquatic, tribal	D	1-10
5	Bandit	1D6	1	4	120	20% magic arms	N/E	Take prisoners	A	1-6
6	Zombie	1D8	2	8	40	Immune to Charm/Sleep / Silent Movement	N	Undead, guards	*	2-12
7	Berzerker	1D8x2	1+1	7	120	+2 hit / Never surrender or retreat	N	No prisoners	J	1-10
8	Kobold	1D4	1/2	7	60	Saves at +3	LE	Ambush, traps	J	2-20
9	Human Cleric	1D8	1-3 (D8)	7-5	120	Spells / Arms	G	Holy warriors	A	1-3
10	Orc	1D6	1	7	90	Attacks at -1 in sun	CE	Tribal, hostile	D	1-10
11	Dwarf Figher	1D8	1-3 (D10)	4-2	80	25% magic arms/armor	N/G	Sturdy fighters	G	1-3
12	Troglodyte	1D4x3	2	5	120	S1-4; Save vs. poison -6str/ round	CE	Loathes humans	A	1-2
13	Human Fighter	1D8	1-3 (D10)	3-1	90	Arms, armor / 20% magic	N/G	Strong, heroes	A	1-3
14	Halfling Thief	1D6	1-3(D6)	9-7	90	Backstab x2 / Hide 20% Magic	N/G	Stealth, small	A	1-3
15	Fire Beetle	2D8	1+2	4	120	Two glands light / 10´ radius/1D6 days	N	Nocturnal, unintelligent	*	2-5
16	Huge Spider	1D6	2+2	6	180	Save vs. poison at +1; / Surprise 1-5	N	Trap-door hunters	J, N, Q	1-2
17	Ghoul	1d3x3	2	6	90	Touch: save vs. paralyzation	CE	Bestial scavenger	B	1-6
18	Large Spider	1	1+1	8	60	Save vs. poison at +2	N	Large webs	J, N	1-4
19	Giant Ant	1D6	2	3	180	Treasure in egg chamber / +type S	N	Nest, builders	Qx3	2-5
20	Human Magic-User	1D6	1-3	10	120	Spells, staff, sling	N/G	Magic	A	1-3
21	Gnoll	2D4	2	5	90	Leaders are 3HD/16hp	CE	Dislike work	D	1-8
22	Skeleton	1D6	1	8	70	Immune to Charm/Sleep / Silent Movement	N	Undead, guards	*	1-4
23	Gnome Illusionist	1D6	1-3	10	120	Spells/darts/staves	N/G	Magic	C	1-3
24	Yellow Mold	0	2*	*	*	2HD/10´hit. 50% chance of spores / save vs. poison	----	Immobile, asphyxiates	*	1-2
25	Goblin	1D6	1-1	6	90	Attacks at -1 in sun	LE	Attack dwarves	L	1-6
26	Elf Fighter / Magic User	1D8	1-3	6-4	120	Spells, arms, armor	N/G	Magical fighters	E	1-3
27	Green Slime	0	2	*	0	Only hurt by fire/cold	N	Immobile, drops	*	1-2
28	Shadow	1D4	2+2	7	90	Hit -1 STR Need magic to hit / Immune to Charm/Sleep	L/E	Intelligent, immaterial	L	1-4
29	Giant Centipede	1pt.	1/4	9	150	Save vs. poison +4	N	Aggressive	*	1-6
30	Wererat	1D6	3	7	120	Requires silver/magic to hit	N/E	Sly	C	1-6

DXT=Damage X Attack / HD=Hit Dice / AC=Armor Class / MV=Movement / AL=Alignment / TD=Temperament or Disposition / TT=Treasure Type / APP=Number Appearing

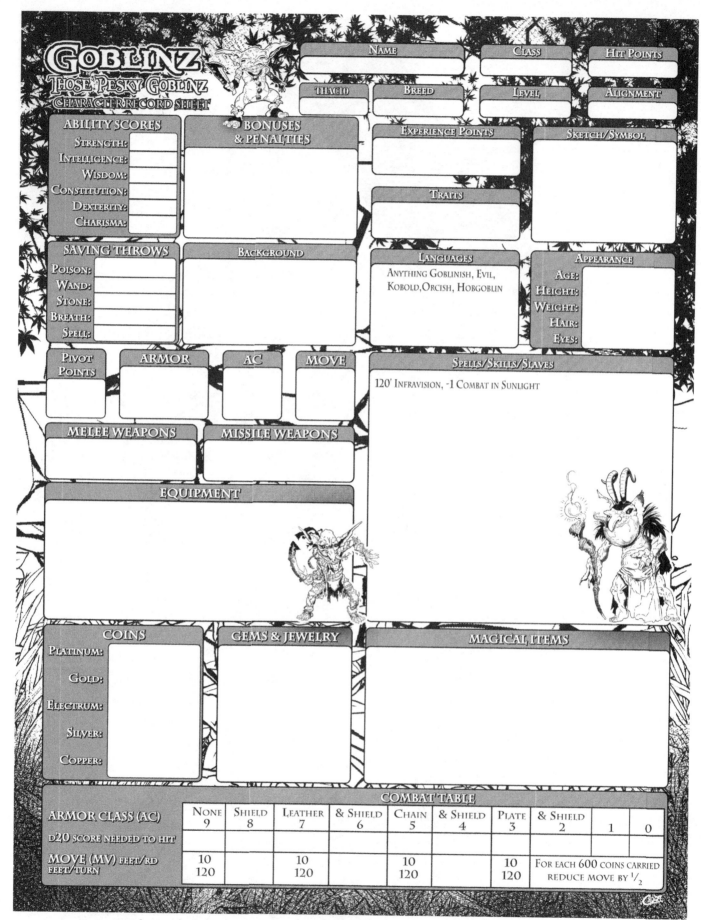

Those Pesky Goblinz

Dungeon Module GZ1
Raid on Morrus
by Justin LaNasa
Based on works by Vince "Evil DM" Florio

TSR Hobbies, LLC.
Lake Geneva, WI 53147

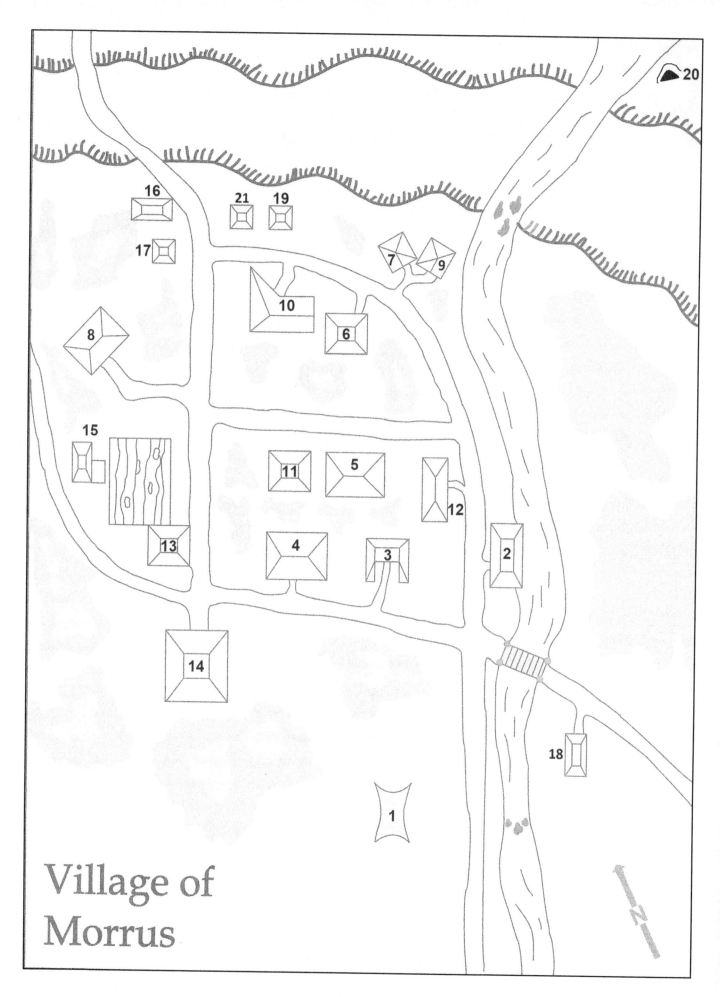

Goblin Chief Therious wants you goblinz to raid Morrus for supplies, loot, magic components, and anything else not strapped down. But you must do this in silence, because, as low-level goblinz you could be captured or killed! Go during the night and be as stealthy as possible. If the village is alarmed by your presence, you could be quickly overwhelmed.

Therious will send 2D4 regular goblinz with you as support.
 Goblinz: AL: LE, AC: 6 HP: 1-7, #AT 1 DMG 1-6 or by weapon type, 4 ft tall, THAC10 (11)
Therious says there is one thing that he will reward the goblinz generously for if brought back in one piece. A magic stine. It is located somewhere in the town. (It is a silver stine with marvelous figures of bare women carved embossment around the mug). The goblinz are to be told to exit the goblinz lair at midnight on a warm summer night at location 20.

History
Morrus is a simple village near the river, getting its main water from the river and most of its food source(fish). There is nothing fancy about the village as it has smoothed dirt paths as its "roads" and there are trees and bushes scattered throughout the village giving it its wonderful cozy charm.

The river stretches up north to the Morrus' sister village, Midus, which is similar in its ways, sharing the water supply. The water in this river is considered a "freshwater" supply.

The Red Hand Cult is using a curse to slowly poison the water supply, making people sick. It is a slow and painful death. When someone dies from the curse, their soul is absorbed into a "demonic crystal". Once filled with enough souls, this crystal will be used in a ceremony to summon the Demon Abaddon back to this dimension. The crystal is in a hidden location elsewhere in the world.

The water supply is essential here as both villages share the exact source of water, which trickles down from deep inside the mountains. Inside the mountains, the PCs will get their first glance at the Cult, also known as the Red Hand of Abaddon.

The Curse: The Curse from the Red Hand Cult does not affect goblinz. The goblin tribe the PC's are from has no alliance with the Red Hand Cult but has a "no attack" agreement with cultists. They tend not to work together due to racial differences but will if in a life-and-death situation.

The Goblin Master should roll for human encounters once every five rounds throughout the adventure (1 on a D6) unless an alarm is sounded.

Wandering Encounters:
Roll 1D8
1-2 - 1D3 Elves / AC 6, HP 7, Dmg 1-8 long sword/1-6 bow, THAC10 (11)
3-4 - 1D3 Dwarfs / AC 6, HP 13, Dmg 1-6 hammer, THAC10 (11)
5-6 - 1D3 Guards / AC 5, HP 8, Dmg 1-8 long sword, THAC10 (11)
7-8 - 1D4 Human commoners / AC 9, HP 7, Dmg 1-6 club, THAC10 (11)

Treasure for each encounter will be one roll on the random loot chart.

At night all buildings will be shuddered up, and doors and windows locked from the inside, except for the tavern/inn. Keep that in mind with waking up sleeping residents. All houses have a dinner/alarm bell outside.

1. Burning Pires
When the PCs approach this area, they will see the smoke and fires slowly burning out for what was once a funeral pyre. As they get closer, they can smell flesh burning. (Goblinz can find plenty of human parts and components for their goblin magic and plenty of food large enough for a raiding party. This should look like a giant buffet to the goblinz party).

Average Villager
   Human 0 Level - AL: Varies, Atr: 10/9/9/10/12/9, AC: 10 HP 4, #AT 1, DMG 1-4, THAC10 (11) The average villager is like many in the world and can offer little to no help as to what is happening to their village. (GM play as desired)

2. Fisherman
This is a fish shop, as it's next to the river. The owner, Folie, is a salty hard-headed old dwarf who doesn't like strangers that come into this hometown, especially those that do not bother to buy anything.
   Folie: 3rd level fighter, male dwarf, AL: CN, Atr: 17/9/9/12/16/12, AC: 7, HP: 25 #AT 1 DMG 1-6+1 sword or net save vs. petrification on a hit or trapped 2-5 rounds, THAC10 (9)
Belongings: Leather armor, short sword, net, shield
House contents: 1 roll on a random loot chart.

3. Healers Shop - Miss Millie's Health and Growth Shop
Miss Millie is a kind, old human woman. She is in her late '60s and is friendly and very motherly. She will be very gracious and helpful to humans but may strike a deal with goblinz if the opportunity arises. Her shop appears sparse; there are only a few jars here and there, along with other items listed below for sale.
   Miss Millie: 4th level cleric, female human, AL: NG, AC 1 via a Ring of Protection+4 HP 26 #AT 1 DMG 1-6 via mace, THAC10 (7)
Suggested spells: 1st level: Purify Food and Drink, Magic Stone, Invisibility to Undead. 2nd Level: Aid, Dust Devil.

Miss Millie will have spells per the GM's needs if the players attack and kill her and try to take her ring. Little do they know it was a gift from her deity and will turn into a ring of cursing if removed from her finger. The ring, once placed on a player's finger, adheres to it and causes the player to suffer a -4 to all hit rolls. The only way remove it is to have a cleric of at least 7th level cast a Dispel Curse on it.
Belongings: chain mail, shield, hammer, 10 ft. pole, belladona sprig, belt pouch (large), garlic bud, Holy Symbol (wood), bullseye lantern, rations (iron), spike, and a water skin.
House contents: 2 Potions of Healing (1d4 pts), 1 Potion of Healing (1d6 pts) and 10 Healing Salves (1 Hp), a potion (worthless to humans goblinz heroism), and 3 rolls on random loot chart.

4. General Store
This is a primary general store; The shop is owned by a human couple, Deemus and Lucie.
   Deemus: 2nd level fighter, male human, AL: CG, Atr: 15/10/9/12/13/10, AC: 5 HP: 12, #AT 1 DMG 1-8, THAC10 (10)
   Lucie: female human 2nd level monk, female human, AL: LN, Atr: 15/15/15/15/15/15. AC: ? HP: 8, #AT 1, DMG 1-4, THAC10 (10)
Deemus belongings: Long sword, chain mail
Lucie belongings: Robes
House contents: 4 rolls on a random loot chart.

5. The Silver Sail Inn & Brewery

There is a large canvas sail, old and tattered, with a silver sheen over a small front porch. Under the sail are several empty tables and chairs. This Inn has a few private rooms (1 gp per night) and a general room for anyone to sleep in for five coppers a night. The place is owned by a dwarven family, the owner Gornar Rockhammer and his wife, Nola.

The Food & Drink:
Beverages
Wine List
- House Sauvignon Blanc
  A house-made white wine with flavors that are full and green.
  Bottle Price: 3 sp
  Glass price: 3 cp

Lagers & Ales
- Yellow Zombie Porter
  5% ABV
  A micro-brewed brown porter. She was described as a complex porter with a smooth finish.
  Gallon Price: 1 sp
  Pint price: 6 cp

Liquors
- House Vodka
  A house-made potato vodka.
  Bottle Price: 2 sp
  Shot price: 10 cp

Food Menu
Starters
- Stuffed Green Peppers
  A platter of green peppers stuffed with a piece of cream cheese and potato concoction: 2 cp
- Soups & Salads: 2 cp
- Fish Stew
  A smooth stew with small chunks of fish and cubed potatoes: 2 cp
- Grilled Chicken and Romaine Salad
  Leaves of romaine tossed with onions. It was topped with grilled chicken: 3 cp

Entrees
- Stewed Turkey
  Stewed turkey on a bed of quinoa: 4 cp

Note: Consuming raw or undercooked meats, poultry, seafood, shellfish, or eggs may require a constitution saving throw for humans, but not for goblinz.

Gornar: 4th level fighter, male dwarf AL: CG, Atr: 13/9/10/15/12,/10, AC: 9, HP: 21, #AT 1, DMG: 1-6+1, THAC10 (7)

Nola: 3rd level thief, female dwarf, AL: LN, Atr: 15/15/15/15/15/15, AC: 9, HP: 15, #AT 1, DMG: 1-4+1, THAC10 (9)

Gornar belongings: Gornar's Ale Stine (magic) Faintly glows when orcs are within a 100-foot radius and with a faint red glow if female. Short Sword Quality +1 nonmagical, street clothes.
Nolas belongings: Dagger, robes, Dagger +1
House contents: 3 rolls on a random loot chart, large chest with 250 cp, 180 sp, 45 gp, trapped (needle save vs. poison or die).

6. Blacksmith

This is a blacksmith shop; the owner is Seather, is a male dwarf. He also appears sick, but this is only because he drinks nothing but ale and is drunk most of the time. He is a great blacksmith, but only when sober. He will appear to be confident when he is drunk, his weapon-making skills falter, and any weapon he has made while drunk may look and feel great when picked up, but will fall apart upon the first hit in battle. They will break in half when used with forceful hits. Should any PC take a weapon or armor from this smith, there is a 20% chance each round it will fall apart or break.

Seather: 3rd level fighter, male dwarf, AL: CN, Atr: 16/10/8/12/17/8, AC: ?, HP: 21, #AT 1, DMG: 1-8+2, THAC10 (9)

Belongings: Chain mail/ helm /Battle Axe +1
House contents: 1 roll on a random loot chart,

2 long swords, 2 short swords 1 battle axe, 5 daggers, 1 silver bladed dagger, 1 small shield, 1 large shield, 1 chain mail, 20 Iron Spikes, and 5 sets of horseshoes

7. Fitch's Hut

This hut is Fitch's home, and if the PCs want to go to investigate, they will find out its just an average place. There is nothing unusual about it that would make it stand out. It appears to be abandoned and vacant. The door will be locked the home and windows shudders will be locked from the inside. There are also boards outside the doors and windows as the house has been closed off to the public.

Fitch's wife and child left the village to live with her mother. If the players want to enter Fitch's hut, they will have to break open the wood to get in. Once they remove a piece of the wood, they will be able to catch a glimpse of what's inside. The home appears to have light coming from inside, and some furniture is overturned and broken. There is a foul smell of death in the home.

Once inside, if they go in the bedroom area, the PCs will find some old rags that have blood on them. The dried up bones of what was obviously Fitch lie on the bed half covered in a foul-smelling blanket.

Fitch will spring from his fallen space, surprising anyone on a 1-4 on a D6, PCs can conclude that this is where Fitch spent his last hours
Players will find a note that seems to be written in the hand of a woman. Read the following to the players if any can read common.
"My dear Fitch has died. The sickness took him so fast, his suffering was too much to bear. To watch him go into his deep sleep, and then awake and become so vile and evil, attacking everyone who tried to help him...I pray that his soul finds peace on his journey to the gods..."

Fitch: undead skeleton, AL: N, AC: 7, HP: 8 #AT 1 DMG 1-6 suffers half damage from sharp weapons, THAC10 (11)
Belongings: A amulet with a drawing of his wife and child.
House contents: 2 rolls on a random loot chart.

8. School

This building serves as a school for the young children in town, and it's run by a human female named Nancy. She is in her mid-forties.
Nancy: 2 level magic-user, female human, AL: LG, Atr: 10/14/14/12/13/10 AC: ?, HP: 7 #AT 1 DMG 1-4, THAC10 (10), she has Magic Missile memorized
Nancy's belongings: Dagger, dress, spellbook with Magic Missile and Comprehend Languages.
House contents: 1 roll on a random loot chart.

9. Roger's Hut

This is the same as Fitch's hut, except that Rogers and his wife have just turned into skeletons. The door to the home will be locked, and the shuttered windows will be locked from the inside. The PCs must break open the door or pick a lock to get in.
Roger & Milly: AC: 7 HP 7,5, AL: N, #AT 1 DMG 1-6 suffers half damage from sharp weapons, THAC10 (11)
Belongings: Nothing of value unless you want human bones.
House contents: 1 roll on a random loot chart.

10. Village Hall

This is a village hall where the villagers will meet to discuss issues. The mayor's office is located here as well. The mayor appears to be out of town on business. When the players enter the building, they will be attacked by 4 Human Zombies.

Zombies: AC 8 HP 12 #AT 1 DMG 1-8 AL N, THAC10 (10)
Belongings: 4 short swords, 3 leather pouches, and a tinder box.
House contents: 2 rolls on a random loot chart.

11. Small Guard Hut

This is basically where the guard on duty will stay and sleep. Currently, there is one guard on duty named Youngerman.

Younderman: 2nd level fighter, human male AL: NG, Atr. 13/8/8/12/8/9 AC: 5 HP: 12 #AT 1 DMG 1-6, THAC10 (10)
Belongings: Short sword, leather pouch, tinder box, chain mail.
House contents: 1 roll on a random loot chart.

12. Undertaker

This is where the undertaker lives, and no one knows his name. He only goes by "The Undertaker".

Undertaker: 3rd level fighter, male human, AL: CN, Atr: 15/10/10/12/13/10, AC: ?, HP: 12 #AT 1 DMG 1-6, THAC10 (10)
Belongings: 24 coffins, 100 nails, hammer, dagger.
House contents: 1 roll on a random loot chart.

13. Don's Odd Things

This is a shop full of various trinkets and good luck charms. Only crazy people believe in this kind of stuff; Don comes across as a sleazy, inbred, snake oil salesman. None of his items work, and all are a sham. His favorite quote is, "There's a sucker born every day!"

Donald O'Smiley: 4th level thief, male human, AL: CN, Atr: 12/13/12/12/13/17, AC: 8 HP: 15, #AT 1 DMG 1-6, THAC10 (7)
Belongings: 10 rabbits feet, 1 cavity-laden dragon tooth, 2 Fairy Dusts, a rusty short sword, and leather armor with suspicious stains on the backside of the trousers.
House contents: 2 rolls on a random loot chart.

14. Mayors Hut

This is the home of the town mayor, Thomas De Marco. He is out of town on official business, though he told no one what the business was. The place is locked up well, but should the PCs want to break in, allow it. The hut is furnished

with what is only considered the best in town, from paintings to little statues made of what appears to be gold and Many tapestries of quality hanging from the walls. There are 10 of these and are very heavy. Hidden in his bedroom will be 6 gems x50 gp, and 400 gold pieces. In a large chest (Trapped unless command word is spoken (Marco's Gold), a Lightning Bolt spell will activate, striking all in front of the chest doing 6d6 save for half). There are four guards here.

Guards: 2nd level fighters, male humans, AL: LN, AC 5 HP 8,7,10,11 #AT 1 DMG 1-8, THAC10 (10)
Belongings: 4 sets of chain mail and four long swords.
House contents: 2 rolls on a random loot chart.

15. Woodcutter/Mill

Helisachar: 2nd level cleric, male dwarf, AL: LN, Atr: 14/13/16/11/12/8, AC: 3, HP: 5, THAC10 (10)
Secondary Skill: Carpenter/Mason
Belongings: Banded mail, shield, flail, club, 50 ft. rope, ale, iron box (large), iron box (small), lantern (hooded), and a wax candle.
Personality: Ruthless, clever, and mean.
Suggested Spells: Cure Light Wounds and Command.
House contents: 1 roll on a random loot chart. Inside the house, you will find a woodcutters axe.

16. Church
Sigismund: 3rd level cleric, male human, AL: LN, Atr: 14/8/17/16/16/14, AC: 6, HP: 18, THAC10 (9)
Secondary Skill: gambler
Belongings: leather, shield, staff, Flail+3, chest, Holy Symbol (wood), mead, prayer beads, quiver, spike, tallow candle, and tinder box.
Personality: Unpredictable, weird, and unscrupulous.
Suggested spells: 1st Level: Magic Stone, Create Water. 2nd Level: Find Traps.
House contents: 1 roll on a random loot chart and a locked chest containing 100 cp, 50 sp, and 25 gp.

17. Mason
Hernegliscus: 3rd level fighter, male half-elf, AL: CG, Atr: 12/10/6/9/9/16, AC: 5, HP: 23, THAC10 (9)
Secondary Skill: mason/carpenter
Belongings: scale mail, shield, quarterstaff, hand axe, 50 ft. rope, bone case (map/scroll), 2 x Lantern (bullseye), 2 x wax candle
Personality: Moody, miserly, and honorable.
House contents: 1 roll on a random loot chart, and trowel, a hammer, a chisel, brushes, and a square.

18. Tailor & Cobbler
Tawhaki: 2nd level fighter, female halfling, AL: LN, Atr: 11/11/5/11/13/11, AC: 3, HP: 8, THAC10 (10)
Secondary Skill: trader/Tailor/Cobbler
Belongings: Banded mail, shield, longbow, light crossbow, belt pouch (large), iron box (large), 2 bullseye lanterns, silver mirror, wax candle, and some wine.
Personality: Hedonistic and perceptive
House contents: 1 roll on a random loot chart.

19. Bakehouse
Lamus: 4th level fighter, human male, AL: NG, Atr: 15/14/13/12/15/12, AC: 4, HP: 20, THAC10 (7)
Secondary Skill: Baker
Belongings: banded mail, long sword, battle axe, 10 ft. pole, flask of Holy Water, Holy Symbol (iron), iron box (large), mirror (metal), and a tallow candle

Personality: garrulous, disturbed, and pious
House contents: 1 roll on a random loot chart.

20. Goblinz Lair Entrance
This entrance is hidden by foliage and rocks. The only way you know its there is if you know or you're a goblin. It would be the same as detecting a secret door 1 in 6 on a D6 if looking for the entrance. Only elves and druids might have a natural chance of discovering when passing nearby.

21. Money Changer
This small building is ran by a gnome named Qwerty. He is a fast-talker and a clever barterer. He loves to underpay for gems and resell them at a higher rate. His son, Wert, is always with him.
Qwerty: 2nd level thief, male gnome, AL: CG, Atr: 11/11/13/14/14/16, AC: 7, HP: 13, THAC10 (10)
Secondary Skill: gambler
Belongings: Leather armor, short sword, short bow, bone case (map/scroll), 2 x wax candle
Personality: Happy, charming, and deceiving.
Shop contents: 3 rolls on a random loot chart.
Wert: 1st level illusionist, male gnome, AL: CG, Atr: 8/14/10/16/13/14, AC: 6, HP: 4, THAC10 (11)
Spells: Phantasmal Force
Belongings: Leather armor, dagger, short bow.

Random Loot D100

#	Item	#	Item
1	Heirloom broadsword, plain but quality. An unknown script runs along the inner side of the scabbard.	51	A holy symbol (Odin).
2	Floppy green hat.	52	Halfling-made gardening tools. Trowel, fork, rake, seed hole spike.
3	100' feet of rope.	53	A masons hammer.
4	Jug of pickled eggs and beets.	54	A hand saw.
5	A healing ointment. It heals 2HP per application. Five applications.	55	A set of four chisels.
6	A black sock full of sling stones.	56	A scroll tube containing the deed to a house in the town of Midus.
7	A small puppy dog.	57	A tiny jar of glitter night dust. (a narcotic)
8	A cursed scroll (GM's choice)	58	A roll of ten torches.
9	A short bow and quiver of ten arrows.	59	A sack of dry beans.
10	A prayer book to Thor.	60	A poisonous snake.
11	A ratty kilt, but comfy.	61	A bundle of eight bow staves. (unfinished)
12	A wooden flute.	62	A bag of apple seeds.
13	An extra pair of boots.	63	Flint and steel fire starter set.
14	Jug of good mead.	64	A bottle of perfume.
15	A small black hooded cloak with six inside pockets.	65	Forty feet of steel wire on a spindle.
16	A golden signet ring, origin unknown.	66	A camp knife.
17	A dwarven mug. May use a weapon, 1D4 dam.	67	A game of stones with a cloth board.
18	Ten sticks of chalk.	68	A piglet.
19	A hide of fine leather.	69	A pack mule.
20	A dozen hard sausages.	70	A heavy wool blanket.
21	A five-gallon cask of brandy.	71	A wax paper packet of blue dye powder.
22	Four javelins.	72	A pair of bear fur knee breeches.
23	A wood staff.	73	A straw broom.
24	A dried ham.	74	A high-quality sharpening stone.
25	A spear.	75	A bolt of undyed linen.
26	A set of four horseshoes.	76	Large silver mirror.
27	An ink pot, quills, and sheaf of paper.	77	A small sundial on a necklace.
28	A small bag of salt and a small bag of pepper.	78	Folies five-page guide to mustaches and beards.
29	A sewing kit.	79	A six-inch crystal lens.
30	A dozen 12-hour candles.	80	A small silver mirror.
31	A small soapstone carving of a horse. (non-magical)	81	A large loaf of tasty bread.
32	A large leather sack.	82	A Ring of Luck, +1 on all saves, roll again on this list.
33	A pound of deer jerky.	83	A fishing pole with a line and hook.
34	Father's old round shield (medium).	84	A tortoise shell hair comb.
35	A map of the kingdom.	85	A bird net.
36	A bundle of letters to be delivered.	86	A copper tongue scraper.
37	A metal hoe.	87	A pair of heavy leather gloves.
38	A huntsman's horn.	88	A bag of candied fruits.
39	A small leather drum.	89	A tiny baby sleeping in a crib.
40	A troll's hand mounted on a three-foot rod. It will grasp objects or make a fist. Commands, grab it, let go, fist. Beware (The troll may regenerate fully within weeks (Note to GM).	90	A Wand of Charm, 2 charges.
41	A bestiary. This book allows the player to ask a question of the GM about any creature listed in his books. (If player can read common)	91	An excellent sheppard's pie.
42	A broad belt with bronze plates.	92	A large bar of hard soap.
43	A long stem pipe and bag of pipe weed.	93	A cow.
44	A hand axe and belt sheath.	94	A fine fighting axe +1 to hit.
45	A stone fire pot.	95	A small bag of uncut semi-precious stones (GM's Choice).
46	A wooden lute.	96	A dozen glow wasps in a round wire cage with a handle. Equal to torchlight at night. Requires food and water daily.
47	A lovely squash.	97	A scroll of sheet music.
48	A sack of nuts.	98	A bag of knives and tools.
49	A large copper pot.	99	A quart of honey.
50	A full-face, metal mask, devil-likeness.	100	Dice.

Are you looking for a place to purchase your favorite fantasy books, games, music, or more? Look no further than the Dungeon Hobby Shop Museum in Lake Geneva, Wisconsin! This is the very building where E. Gary Gygax formed TSR and launched the Dungeons and Dragons game role-playing system that changed the world!

The museum is a great place to visit and see where it began. You can even play games there as well. Not only can you see all the versions of D&D from the past, but you can pick up new games like Dungeon Crawl! New products are arriving all the time! The museum is a must for gamers who want to see D&D's past, present, and future!

www.tsrmuseum.com
DHSM:Facebook:www.facebook.com/TSRHobbiesMuseum
TSRConFacebook:www.facebook.com/TSRCON

MAKE RELIVING THE PAST PART OF YOUR FUTURE!

Made in the USA
Monee, IL
13 February 2023

27744313R00031